The Neptune Room

The Neptune Room

Bertrand Laverdure

Translated by Oana Avasilichioaei

LITERATURE IN TRANSLATION SERIES
BOOK*HUG PRESS 2020

FIRST ENGLISH EDITION

Published originally under the title: *La chambre Neptune* © 2016
by La Peuplade, Saguenay, Canada
English translation copyright © 2020 by Oana Avasilichioaei

LIBRARY AND ARCHIVES CANADA CATALOGUING IN PUBLICATION

Title: The Neptune room / Bertrand Laverdure ; translated by Oana Avasilichioaei.
Other titles: Chambre Neptune. English
Names: Laverdure, Bertrand, 1967– author. | Avasilichioaei, Oana, translator.
Series: Literature in translation series.
Description: First English edition. | Series statement: Literature in translation series |
    Translation of: La chambre Neptune.
Identifiers: Canadiana (print) 2020024311X | Canadiana (ebook) 20200243128

ISBN 9781771665810 (softcover) | ISBN 9781771665827 (EPUB)
ISBN 9781771665834 (PDF) | ISBN 9781771665841 (Kindle)

Classification: LCC PS8573.A815 C4313 2020 | DDC C843/.54—dc23

PRINTED IN CANADA

The production of this book was made possible through the generous assistance of
the Canada Council for the Arts and the Ontario Arts Council. Book*hug Press also
acknowledges the support of the Government of Canada through the Canada Book
Fund and the Government of Ontario through the Ontario Book Publishing Tax
Credit and the Ontario Book Fund.

 **Canada Council
for the Arts** **Conseil des Arts
du Canada**

 ONTARIO ARTS COUNCIL
CONSEIL DES ARTS DE L'ONTARIO
an Ontario government agency
un organisme du gouvernement de l'Ontario

 Funded by the
Government
of Canada Financé par le
gouvernement
du Canada | **Canadä**

 ONTARIO | ONTARIO
CREATES | CRÉATIF

Book*hug Press acknowledges that the land on which we operate is the traditional
territory of many nations, including the Mississaugas of the Credit, the Anishnabeg,
the Chippewa, the Haudenosaunee and the Wendat peoples. We recognize the
enduring presence of many diverse First Nations, Inuit and Métis peoples and are
grateful for the opportunity to meet and work on this territory.

for Aimée Lévesque
and for my dear mother

Life is every person's means of getting through solitude.
CARLOS LISCANO

Reality is that which,
when you stop believing in it,
doesn't go away.
PHILIP K. DICK

Contents

Sandrine, there is no god, no soul. We all conceal thousands of plants, a hundred thousand stalks that sprout, wither, and die. The self's militant bees get lost in the melee of our garden. Some forget to pollinate their choices. Our piece of earth turns back into humus with a determination that is always beyond us. You are a trillion cells looking for light, a colony of organic beings struggling to breathe, live, wilt in the fields, and shrivel from use.

Tiresias is talking to Sandrine, who's drugged up and asleep. She lies on a soft bed whose comfort she can no longer appreciate. Once the appropriate derivative of morphine has been administered, the doctor comes to see her, tell her buttressing stories, like a modern-day Scheherazade, short breviaries of fine wisdom to confront the constant wasting away of her organs.

Every end of life is a bleak or gracious tale, told by a distant doctor.

Here, in palliative care, fatherless, motherless, Sandrine is a land ceded to calamities. She's in the Emily Dickinson Home, a hospice that takes in terminally ill children.

And in a few hours, the last agonizing breath of an eleven-year-old child.

Eric Berthiaume in his car, 2006

In the world of 2006, the immutable might have come in
the guise of Johnny Depp's love for Vanessa Paradis, the
life of Gaétan Soucy, Christina Aguilera, the Charest government, the anonymity of Julian Assange, Carla Bruni
before Sarkozy, the Orange Julep on Sherbrooke, and Eric
Berthiaume's health.

We all go through flat stages in our lives where everything is weightless.

For a moment, which could last several years, our vision constructs a politico-cultural landscape that seems
permanent. It is natural for our brain to produce this
strange illusion. Because our bodies have been designed
to forget the chaos and invent comforting cultural references.

Eric Berthiaume was in his 2003 Subaru, driving on
Route 116 toward Richmond. He was happy as a TV researcher, satisfied with his work environment, which was
stimulating without being rigid, and always took perverse
pleasure in challenging himself. Content with his fate, his
paycheque, the type of show to which he was contributing, his role as a father, still in love with his girlfriend, he
was clearly going through a flat stage cradled in the illusion of the immutable. What's more, wherever he went,
he lugged around the lighthearted, carefree attitude we

tend to confuse with the dangerously incarcerating concept of "happiness."

He was floating. But on what? In what material? On what surface?

Eric Berthiaume, nervous, edgy, son of Syntonie Hundon married to Thorgal Berthiaume from Saint-Félix-de-Kingsey, young father of Sandrine Berthiaume-Côté, sped along Route 116 toward Richmond. Sandrine was five. The sky was clearer than most poetry. The road disappeared as quickly as it appeared; all was well in the realm of benign indifference. The horizon was flat, contained. In the hopscotch of life, no one in the Berthiaume-Côté family had yet stepped on the lines. Chance still whistled its mocking tune in an old Bourvil film.

The car's interior, artfully finished, inspired the most conventional cheerfulness. It was just before noon. The heat cooed like a mourning dove. The asphalt patiently eroded Eric's tires. The belated father listened to Vanessa Paradis on the CD player. "Always the same theme, tandem, ditto." The Gainsbourgian album recorded by this Lolita of the taxi lay in ambush in the CD player of a car speeding toward the Gainsborough landscape.

All was well in the best of worlds.

Ninelle Côté at the same time

At the same time, Ninelle Côté, a Baroque cellist in a mystified Montreal and Eric Berthiaume's partner, is struggling with an arrangement. Her left eye carries the patina of those who know they are better than others. Hierarchies are bizarre concoctions that nature provides to justify our annoyances. Yet the only hierarchy that could exist ought to begin with the Big Bang. Are you before or after the Big Bang, sir? Madam, do you come from the same split atoms as me or are your origins unknown to me, galactically speaking? There would be no hierarchy if everyone based their charter of rights and freedoms on our universe's threshold of existence.

Ninelle is tense, the string of her bow just as agitated as her. She has suffered several intense bouts of depression; the musician wasn't born under the same star as her lover. It's well-known that optimists get into bed with cynics.

Love is brought on by the virus of memory, which is utterly rampant. An instrument of coercion amply reinforced by endorphins, it makes our sojourn on Earth, which Marguerite Yourcenar calls "the prison," temporarily sugar-sweet.

An odd couple, this union of opposite forces should have led to a failed household. Yet all opposites strive to reproduce this very thing: their attraction. The outcome: a child has emerged from the mesh of this net.

On Montreal's streets, Sandrine rides her bike, runs on all fours. She has friends and plays pickup sticks.

On the morning of 2006, on the 116 toward Richmond, Eric looks beyond the windshield, touches the steering wheel, presses on the accelerator.

The road is empty. Vanessa keeps singing.

Tiresias and Pollini's hands, 2006

Tiresias stretches out on her dusky rose armchair.

Her workday is done. That's the official story anyway, since a doctor is never done with others' suffering. When a doctor isn't treating someone, practising medicine, explaining medical concepts in layman's terms, we administer reproof taken right off the internet. We want to understand, and the answers are everywhere. In milliseconds, they burst in from all sides. The great brain of the network, used to consoling the most ingrained solitudes, auscultates all the atoms in our bodies.

A geek like all her patients but for different reasons, Tiresias is never without her iPod U2. As a young medical student at the Université de Montréal, she learned to juggle everyone's fears and positive biases. On the outside, a doctor looks like everyone else. Yet as a traffic officer of anxiety, a doctor is posted at the crossroads of humanity.

In our programmable and programmed civilization, only machines command our respect now, and everyone has gradually forgotten the pretentious need of human infallibility. Tiresias puts up with the normal fallibility of human beings. As she often tells herself, managing death first means dealing with survivors.

On her iPod U2, she selects Chopin's *Études* by Pollini and puts on her earphones. The track is *Étude* No. 3 in E Major. Right from the start, she recognizes the lanky man's scandalous song: "Lemon Incest." Gainsbourg sang this tune, spicing it up with a dance rhythm. A deliberately provocative illustration of an incestuous fantasy: Charlotte, in a duet with her father, responded by propelling her voice/steam in an overheated kettle. The sustained shriek of a lamb looking for her note.

Single, attractive, and in a "many lovers, please" mode, Tiresias doesn't have any children. This situation, rare for a Quebec doctor, doesn't undermine her career whatsoever. Since she can't somatize or introject the loss of a child, she is better prepared, in a way, to bear the final agonies of these broken young plants.

Pollini's hands continue to cross modulated streams over the piano notes. Chopin reminds her that any intelligent person has an educational duty to untangle the composer's meaning for others. This also functions in reverse. Chopin produced complex musical ideas, and now she is partaking in the emotional, unbridled effervescence of a meticulous and grandiloquent fragility. One has to take in the genius and at the same time pierce its mystery. She knows that one day machines will end up understanding the mechanics of fluids. Chaos will be mapped out. We will invent other words to describe it. Tiresias has read about it in *Science and the Future*.

Eric, a deer, his car, 2006

On the road, Eric thinks he sees a deer in the distance.

Then changes his mind; it's really just a stain. Growing larger and larger, the shape now dances on his retina. A violent headache flattens him. His hearing is gone. In his skull, a minuscule blood vessel has just ruptured. A ridiculous glut in a tube no thicker than two sewing threads has just broken the dike. Total collapse, flooding.

The car slows down with almost unreal ease. Behind it, the road is empty for at least a kilometre. The sun shines. Vanessa doesn't know that she's singing a eulogy. No one has invited her.

On the 116 toward Richmond, a Subaru comes to a stop. Eric Berthiaume's last reflex is to press the brake pedal. No airbag inflates. A delicate death on a stretch of smooth asphalt.

A quick death in a burst of happiness.

Birth of Sandrine Berthiaume-Côté, October 2001

Tons of rubble. Tons of sharp tesserae of glass, long faces moulded by the offences of the initiated. Calls for aid, and a country goes to war on the springboard of money.

One month later. October 2001.

Beneath the world's dust, something previously inanimate shakes, a living being, a human, a sprout of particular sex gesticulates. Still, nothing too strange about the beginning of a life, the same as a thousand other births.

Eric Berthiaume has just cut the umbilical cord. Time commences with the exactitude of an awkward carnivore.

Sandrine cries and cries; the great narrative comes and goes, and then the short fiction begins.

Contrary to legend, not all fathers fall in the parturient battle. Eric held his own. Didn't lose consciousness.

The mother suffered, as is her lot, felt the reprehensible damage of a head as enormous as hope. She pulled the train into the station. It's the beginning of the film.

Tiresias and Marthe-Lyster, 2008

Tiresias is asleep.

Sometimes, in the middle of the night, she sheds her breasts and becomes the man she always thought she was. Her sexuality flickers. His sex is random.

Wandering like an old Japanese poet in sandals and a straw hat, Tiresias (now "he") revisits the realm of his difficult loves. Paying the ferryman his dues, he boards the small raft. Talks with the boatman. A young Vietnamese with fiery eyes.

—Are you looking for company?

—I don't know. I'm lost in my own nightmares.

—(*The ferryman insists*) How would you rate your social loss?

—I've been told I'm an eight.

—That's very high. Your neuroses are complex; what's more, you're probably not made for sustained companionship. Do you plan on visiting the museum of your relational horrors?

—My affairs are erratic and so are my relationship problems. I don't have a museum of horrors. My past is terrible because it's painfully banal.

—But by crossing the river of sexuality you are seeking answers to your questions.

—Do we ever do anything else?

The ferry then bangs against the shore. The young boatman gives a start.

In a city where sexuality is no longer an absolute value, a self-definition tipping the balance of accounts or love affairs, Tiresias stretches, almost wakes up, coughing slightly. Connecticut is not a city built by urban planners but rather an amalgam of roundabouts, cul-de-sacs, and winding alleys divided at its centre by the great Missisquoi Boulevard. Lycurgus Street is to the left. The doctor-poet decides to begin his walk there.

Then the streets of Montreal appear. Corner of Jean-Talon and Saint-Hubert. Suddenly, the mood of the dream goes haywire. In the window of a fabric store, the figure of Marthe-Lyster Dessalines greets him with cruel indifference. Tiresias feels an unpleasantness return. Painful rhizomes penetrate his body, which is wracked by a laughable, awkward amorous impulse. He keels over, reaches out his hand, runs on a tarmac soaked in gasoline. Everything is on fire, but the flames don't hurt him. A portly man wearing both a hijab and a kippah seems to be asking him to slow down and sends a squadron of motorcycles after him.

Tiresias sees a mirror and instinctually knows it's a portal to death. He thrusts a foot into the reflecting surface. His body gradually disappears behind the silvering.

*

At a conference on new medical technology and software, Tiresias sets down his wineglass on a coffee table next to a Louis XV loveseat. He doesn't notice, at first, the intriguing programmer sipping a Diet Pepsi. She makes an offhand remark, intended for anyone standing in the vicinity of her voice.

—We'll do everything ourselves soon enough. It won't be long now.

Not understanding, Tiresias asks her to clarify her meaning.

—Soon you'll no longer be necessary. You doctors. If I'm not mistaken, you're a doctor, right?

—How can you tell?

—You were holding your wineglass by the stem and when you set it down, I didn't hear a thing. Your dexterity is excellent.

—That's not a very distinctive characteristic.

—Since we're at a conference of computer scientists and doctors, it's possible to separate the two professions by observing the etiquette. A computer scientist bangs away, a doctor stitches up. The border stands there.

The conversation then flowed of its own accord. The young computer scientist's sharp mind intrigued and seduced him. A programmer of medical computer interfaces, Marthe-Lyster Dessalines explained to him at length that bearing in mind a classic evolutionary scenario, the middleperson would lose their importance in the future. The patient would then take sole control of their healing, using the nanobiological instruments placed at their disposal. By caricaturing the position of doctors in our contemporary societies, she even went so far as to predict that within a century doctors would no longer be any more important than poets.

Struck by such foolish impudence, Tiresias then lectured her on the crucial societal contribution of bards in past centuries, naming a handful of greats, at whose mention she made no reaction. Constantly seeking new poets, he even quoted the title of a poem by Tao Lin that had made a strong impression on him: "A stoic philosophy based on the scientific fact that our thoughts cause our feelings and behaviours."

—Poets are becoming ridiculous philosophers while doctors are slowly becoming poets.

—Your comment is stupid and disingenuous!

The stormy exchange continued unabated until Tiresias was on his sixth glass of wine. The young cynic then placed a surprise kiss on her interlocutor's lips. Seized by the invitation, the doctor unfolded his cinematic arms, grabbed the shrewd woman's neck, and kissed her on the mouth as you would expect.

*

Three months later, the couple were living together in the doctor's condo.

Most relationships begin lion-like. This one more than others, but in general, nature is in a rush. It doesn't take into account the climate or region. Magnetism works just as well in geology as in humanology. No one is immune. No one actually puts up a resistance. Tiresias took hairpin curves with as much skill as he went in tiresome straight lines. But with Marthe-Lyster, he reached unprecedented speeds. Neuropsychologists tell us that our actions are, in a way, preprogramed and our consciousness gives us the impression that we are the ringmaster of this constant circus. Every time we think we will decide what will happen, our body has already beaten us to it. Sometimes by ten minutes, sometimes by three hundred milliseconds. Delayed-action self-awareness. At times, nature, the earth, or any other all-encompassing entity seems to prevail over our will. We then feel predetermined, connected to mysterious laws that govern large groups.

Yet the illusion of our individuality is so rooted in our moral standards that no one understands the fact that an independent mind is a trap. We are networked, predictable, self-aggrandizing. Leaden imitations, we plummet into fiction like everyone else.

In the early hours of a winter day—bagel wolfed down, Kusmi Prince Vladimir tea squeezed into a tea infuser spoon, grapefruit cut lengthwise in slices (easier to skin)—the routine, which is synonymous with "immutable normality," was unfolding accordingly. In bed, the frizzy hair poking out from under the pillow indicated that the mattress was still serving a human body. No blizzard while the sun's out. Not many blizzards in Montreal.

When Marthe-Lyster's eyes grasped the substance of the day, as she raised herself from the sheets, something happened in her cerebral biodome.

She was no longer the same.

Possible causes: the fight of the previous night suddenly took on gigantic proportions; the thoughts about her future, which she'd been pondering secretly for over three weeks, were already having an impact; various scenarios of reorienting herself now seemed necessary; the annoying discovery that it was just a fling had opened her eyes; her lover's hands, less enterprising than three weeks ago, indicated a change in his desire, and she realized that she too had just passed stage three, which culminates in platonic indifference, and didn't want to open the sluice gates of habit any further; a burgeoning and unsettling distress was urging her to plunge back into solitude.

Tiresias felt a neural paradigm shift in his lover's eyes. Sometimes, as though inside a cerebral labyrinth, we have no way of finding the minotaur at the root of our urgent, dumbfounded desire. In fact, we hide thousands of minotaurs inside us, making thousands of decisions affecting our human course, decisions that are final and jump the track of our previous whims.

Less cheerful, though still somewhat playful, Marthe-Lyster suddenly became an actress, a mime, the curtain drawn over the performance unfolding in her mind. He couldn't attribute this attitude to any well-founded cause. He simply smiled, ate with her, gave her a kiss when she left for work, and pretended that nothing had happened in the subsequent hours. Yet something had shifted. Irrevocably. For over a month, in moments of extreme fatigue, when she coped with stress at work by seeking decompensation in their intimacy, she would send him vague breakup messages. Nothing definitive. It would all end in apologies the next day, isolated texts of "I love you," lengthy embraces when he came home at night. Then, one day, a message popped up on his iPhone 3. Dry, empty words that didn't explain anything but at the same time said it all. The magic formula that broke all spells.

Disappointed by the turn of events, Tiresias felt a deep shame that was unlike him. Not having anticipated this outcome, the fact of having hoped to the very last and projected himself into the future with such naïveté offended him. This love affair of barely four months undermined several of his interpersonal convictions and made him doubt himself. As someone who had never before needed to love to such a degree to be with a woman, he became jealous, hateful, and even felt the lover's sidereal melancholy in the absence of the beloved.

Afterwards, of course, he continued to frequent the female sex, but it was only a game: a spoiled child demanding his sugared almond one lonely evening; a health professional looking for a few thrills in a Harlequin novel and the bar of a three-star hotel. He was nothing more than a cliché in episodes. He blamed himself. But what else could he do to claim the last notes of his love requiem? The composer left much to be desired, and the music dragged on. Each dotted note on the score seemed to come from afar and required too much of his time. After several months, he knew he should see a psychologist colleague. But his determination to not show his confusion held him back. In the end, it was only once he had left the hospital and began working full-time at the Emily Dickinson Home, the palliative care centre for children, that he found some kind of solace. No matter, he would become a poet of grief, a doctor who eases pain and talks with his patients. It was clear that poetry, which speaks only of death, is in the spotlight in these contexts where the Grim Reaper is the main screenwriter. With a cynical wink to his ex's joke, and not without feeling fatalist and harsh, he would spend the end of his days comforting ter-

minally ill children. He would become a poet and antici-
pate by a hundred years the loss of social influence of the
College of Physicians. A great farce defending privilege
that he told himself couldn't last *ad vitam æternam*.

Josiane, 2011

The staircase is corroded by rust. On the second floor, the landing looks like a crushed mille feuille.

Josiane hesitates. She's been assigned this apartment, in which a ten-year-old girl suffering from an incurable disease is trying by all possible means to forget her condition. An art education student, Josiane knows this experience is crucial for her internship grade; her report will need to be flawless and conclusive. Before ringing the doorbell, she takes a deep breath. It's awkward to spend time one-on-one. Also, keeping somebody occupied is always a difficult task. Being responsible for a person's activities over a given period of time requires concentration and an ounce of acting talent. She will need to prove that she has the situation under control, knows what she's doing, and all will be well.

Josiane's mind is riddled with anxiety. The door doesn't open right away. The wait drags on. She is reminded of a passage in a book she read for her course. She presses the doorbell one more time and digs through her bag. She finds her notebook, then the quote by philosopher Pierre Zaoui:

> To be sick is to be alive, to be human. And all
> our hyperactive societies today will try to deny
> this by shutting in the sick, the disabled, the

abnormal, "invisiblizing" them in public life, "understating" their private life ("come on, it's not that serious"), and digitizing them into sets of biological parameters and epidemiological statistics, all to no avail: illness always ends up coming back in one's body or that of a loved one like an *existential* prime, as in the a priori category of our existence, our human condition, beyond any politics, any numbers, and any medico-technical discourse.

*

In the living room of this ordinary apartment, there is an immense sofa. Sandrine is lying on it, exhausted.

The first few minutes of interacting with the sick child are difficult. Nevertheless, Josiane does all she can to dispel any unease and make the activity of building a rocket amusing for the girl. Yet her protege remains cold. What if her idea is dumb?

—I like plastic jewellery and lots of other things— books and movies too, Sandrine says, seeing Josiane's bag full of materials. It then feels as though everything will fail peacefully. *Requiescat in pace* for her rocket project made of a paper towel roll, several types of shiny beads, and a conical cup of wax paper. Her attempt to deconstruct the rocket and make a long necklace annoys the young girl even more.

On the soft, faded sofa, Sandrine is bored and lets her know it. Zaoui may have written that in its essence life is unstable and that a sick human being is no doubt more aware of existing than a so-called healthy one, but these ideas don't help her at all at the moment.

Sandrine has already closed her eyes.

The day of the future art education graduate comes to an end.

*

Josiane checks out the Top 10 charts for the week of May 2 to 8, 2011, in *La Presse*:

Top 10 French Albums

1) Ginette Reno, *La musique en moi* (number 3 last week)
2) Marie-Élaine Thibert, *Je suis* (new this week)
3) Richard Desjardins, *L'existoire* (number 1 last week)
4) Marie Denise Pelletier, *Marie Denise Pelletier* (new this week)
5) Boom Desjardins, *Avec le temps* (number 2 last week)
6) Various, *Le retour de nos idoles* (number 13 last week)
7) Vincent Vallières, *Le monde tourne fort* (number 10 last week)
8) Alain Morisod & Sweet People, *Buona sera* (number 6 last week)
9) Lara Fabian, *Je me souviens* (number 7 last week)
10) Michel Louvain, *Je n'ai pas changé* (number 12 last week)

Top 10 English Albums

1) Pascale Picard Band, *A Letter to No One* (new this week)
2) Roch Voisine, *Americana 2* (number 1 last week)
3) Adele, *21* (number 2 last week)
4) Jennifer Lopez, *Love?* (new this week)
5) Nadja, *Everything's Going My Way* (number 3 last week)
6) Beastie Boys, *Hot Sauce Committee Part Two* (new this week)
7) France D'Amour, *Bubble Bath & Champagne* (number 4 last week)
8) Roch Voisine, *Americana* (number 6 last week)
9) Yael Naim, *She Was a Boy* (new this week)
10) Ima, *Precious* (number 8 last week)

On her iPod, she is listening to Richard Desjardins's "Sur son épaule." She doesn't know if *L'existoire* is her favourite album of the year, but the story of the waitress in an all-night diner makes her melancholic. A story similar to that of the robotic waitress in the rock opera *Starmania*. Something about the fragility of time, which passes radiating the life of an isotope of doubt. "But like so many princess / She no longer believes in promises."

Sandrine's case is a bit like this. Promises no longer carry any weight for people who are dying.

*

During her evening walk, Josiane sits on a park bench. An elderly man walking a Lhasa Apso passes in front of her. The fluffy dog looks at her for a moment, then loses interest in her. In the dark vivarium of night, despite the uncertain alleviation of beings and things, everything goes on regardless.

Ninelle, 2007—The last concert

Ninelle Côté is walking in circles in her apartment, watching her daughter. Sandrine invents a fiery game on the tiled floor, calls out to her mother with a voice that rumbles like a pair of drumsticks.

—Look, Mom, the tiles protect me from the fire. You have to jump here and here, or you'll fall into the lava! Look!

Her mother stands in front of a score: *Tombeau de Marais le Père* by Charles Dollé. A composition for viola da gamba, one of the last for this instrument's repertoire, published in 1737 by a composer about whom almost nothing is known. Ninelle will play this piece at Bertrand Lancoignard's soirée. A patron of baroque music, Lancoignard holds an annual concert at his house, inviting the best instrumentalists from the Montreal region. Emulating the example of secret societies, baroque music lovers in Montreal attend a circuit of private concerts in apartments and houses. Lancoignard's soirée is the high point of the underground baroque year.

A harpsichordist will accompany Ninelle. The evening will feature Charles Dollé's work, and singers will interpret other compositions. The wine will flow, and people will also be able to meditate on tatamis in a room set up for this very purpose.

—Please, Sandrine, be quiet. Mom is trying to concentrate here! Go play in your room, OK!

There isn't much conviction in the gambist's tone, parental automatisms exhaled in frustration, warnings without any real threat. The fact that she has to practise a tombeau a few months after Eric's death upsets her. They had told her to change the score, choose another—a gavotte, a dance, something cheerful. But she had insisted: "No, fate has placed an iceberg in my way. I'm not going to refuse a tombeau just so I can artificially cheer myself up."

The lively, spiralling bowings of the first measures followed by a dead stop remind her of the violent cycle of life, full of flourishes and ruptures. A composition that constantly circles around and backtracks, a slow cycle, a funeral composition that seems to carry the burden of the dead body all the way to the altar.

On this evening, it's clear, she will play a tribute to Eric Berthiaume. If she cries in the middle of the concert, it will add to her performance. Her limbs tremble, her fingers crush the strings with restrained fury. Her eyes stare at the notes, which unexpectedly rise and intertwine with dramatic tremolos. Ninelle draws out the note, then thrusts it into a field of possibilities, between human ears, carving her emotion with skill.

The sound of the viola da gamba fills the living room with a crimson, downy softness.

*

Two large rattan chairs made of ebony dominate the centre of the room.

42

Millionaires are eccentric.

Boredom is stuffed with knickknacks.

From atop two black towers that stand as traces of an enormous chess game overlooking the drawing room/concert hall, the singers' voices seep into the ears of the audience—enlightened fans of baroque music—as the hors d'oeuvres of this festive evening.

Ninelle waits in the anteroom of the drawing room. She holds her instrument. She suppresses some sentimental tears threatening to pour out of her eyes that are as exact as programmed vectors.

Her sister helped her to dress. A peculiar sluggishness had taken over her. A sluggishness of disorientation, a sample of distress. She was floundering in confusion. The tunnel of her ego had become a cracked tube broken in many places, through which water leaked and air passed. In this state, reality = a spaghetti plate of useless information.

Ninelle had almost lost the automatisms controlling the muscles that enable us to slip on a sweater and jacket. With pursed lips, her sister had guided the musician's arms through the sleeves, then buttoned up her shirt like a foster mother. It was as though all of Ninelle's faculties now responded only to the stimulus of music.

—Will you be all right, Ninelle?

Taxi. The metronome in her mind. Large doors, the required formalities, polite kisses on cheeks, then a beeline for the bathroom. Next, end up in the place she is now. In the anteroom of the luxurious drawing room, chin held perfectly parallel to the wood floor, neck long and straight.

It's her turn.

She stands up.

Walks towards the drawing room, contaminated by a profusion of notes, advances to the stage, walks around the harpsichord, lands on a black leather chair that's been designated for her.

Applause. Silence. Music.

*

Serene libations, cultivated exchanges, sardonic and good-natured laughter, irony, the post-concert conversations evolve in accordance with the rituals enjoyed by like-minded people. The fans of social distance, the renegades of distinction, the torrent of run-of-the-mill tolerance and elitist biases, all the avatars holding the power relations in place now emit their dark influence, cut the diamond of time along firmly established lines.

Andrew Ductil, a musician and critic for *La Scena Musicale*, brings up his fabulous trip to Croatia. The word surprises, ears perk up, the mood shifts with the rhythm of the piqued curiosity of those present. The city of Split, on Croatia's Adriatic coast, emerges from nothingness in people's minds, starts existing in three dimensions, in memories, in thousand-year-old walls. A city built entirely around the palace of Emperor Diocletian, the persecutor of Christians, Split is now a trendy tourist destination, enticing ravers, young couples, hipsters, and history buffs. Ductil evokes the polyphonic hymns, similar to those sung by Corsicans, of male choruses who show off under the great dome of the ruined cathedral near the harbour. He mentions the tour guides dressed up like Roman soldiers pacing up and down People's Square. Makes one or two jokes about the city's name, delights in the Romans' aversion of Christians, talks about the beaches, the bad wine, the inns where one can meet interesting Europeans.

Then they move on to other things: a musician's new baby, her sick dog, upcoming concerts, encouragements and congratulations circulating among the instrumentalists like natural sugared almonds with a comforting scent, a coded language, the particular happiness of people who have gracefully learned how to play a musical instrument, the enviable cool factor of talented beings.

Ninelle listens without reacting, leaves the drawing room without saying goodbye.

Disappears.

*

Outside, she feels the heaviness of the cold wind. The black plastic case of her instrument is an anthropomorphic landmark with an overly long neck. For a moment, she stands there, aphasic, a member of an immobile duo, married to her instrument.

Then she releases it.

She points her face toward a new source of stupor.

The deserted street in front of the grand Victorian house feels bleak in its tranquility. A quiet street with identical lawns, well-designed sidewalks of concrete basins meticulously striated with brooms by Italian workers; the decor evokes nothing more than a cup of lukewarm coffee on a plastic beige Ikea placemat.

Ninelle contemplates her escape plan.

She walks for twenty minutes before reaching a busy road. Hails a taxi. Opens the car door. Sits down with determination and tells the driver: "Take me to Split, Croatia."

Two hours pass. The partiers leaving Lancoignard's house discover their friend's viola da gamba standing at attention in its rigid case.

The abandoned instrument seems to be waiting for its mistress's deft fingers.

Sandrine, 2009—Illness – One year

Taylor Swift in her bedroom.

The 2009 megahit "You Belong with Me," a song about a teen in love in its most rehashed version. Nevertheless, the pop song still enflames hearts, reaches the emotional satellites of young girls.

Sandrine is eight. She hasn't lived with her mother for over two years. Her aunt Evelyne has become her guardian.

For ten minutes, she's been listening to the conventional song of this mega pop star who will be forgotten in twenty years. The song endlessly repeats, "Why can't you see / You belong with me." But the lyrics are secondary; what matters here is the two-beat tac-a-tac, very square, almost country-western rhythm of this upbeat song. Sandrine is jumping on her bed, out of breath. Overexcited.

The naive realism of parents has never quite grasped the ritualistic essence of these jumping-on-the-bed sessions, when a young human picks up emotions without knowing how to respond, caught in the tangle of their own burgeoning doubts. As an initial first-aid kit of socially acceptable melancholy, hit songs channel the everyday fears and feelings of teens. Since the dosage has never been properly explained, we might criticize children's infatuation with these naive celebrations, yet they remain

47

part of the common hazing ritual that transforms a child into a teen and, eventually, into an adult. Everyone asks for more. Children and parents, in equal doses. There's no point in resisting the melody of time passing, the old trick of the sirens since Greek antiquity, a song of burgeoning pleasures and dawn serenades still to be written; its music is everywhere, and no matter what we say, it will always remain the best laundry line for drying commonplace sorrows.

Sandrine's CD player is set on repeat. Taylor Swift's song continues to pound the walls of her bedroom while her sympathetic aunt finishes doing the laundry.

*

In the schoolyard, a group forms at lunch hour. The game of insults begins. Kids meet up and invent exaggerated insults to make their friends laugh. Sometimes, they are cruel; other times, they sink into the absurd. Either way, laughing is the crucial thing.

Sandrine is playing with Aïsha Riyad in a corner of the yard. All is well until a girl from the group starts laughing and pointing at her. A forced laugh, a satirical laugh that doesn't yet have a name. Sandrine never pays any attention to this bullying and suggests to Aïsha that they go play inside, in the gym. Still, after class, she finds in her slot a lined sheet of paper torn from a binder, bearing three insults aimed at her poor mother. She reads them carefully.

Sandrine's mom is so dumb that when you ask her
what's her sign, she says Stop
Sandrine's mom is so dumb that when she farts, she
thinks someone speaks
Sandrine's mom is so dumb that on garbage day,
she waits for the garbage truck on the sidewalk,
dressed in a garbage bag

Sandrine would like to cry but prefers to laugh, knowing her mother's talent is worth a thousand of these conceited idiots.

She folds the paper and puts it in her pocket.

Sandrine, 2012—Illness + Two years

Two labels printed on a Brother PT-1880 and affixed to the handset and base emphatically indicate the telephone. Each label reads: NEPTUNE CHILDREN.

They've promised her the Neptune Room as of the next day.

The Neptune Room—its name evokes the mythical, fathomless depths of oceans—is intended for children whose suffering will soon end. Welcoming and warm, equipped with an extra bed for family members, this space serves as the last chrysalis.

Sensitivity, supervision, a retreat into an environment that says vacation, this final translation evokes an end lived in optimal conditions.

Evelyne is getting ready to accompany her niece.

The last agony is about to begin.

*

Sandrine stopped eating two days ago. Her condition has worsened.

Tiresias pulls the curtain, lets the sun in, and listens to the slow delirium of the young girl who, despite the intense pain, is gradually unburdening herself of a discernable identity. Our acute desire to determine who we are prevents us from truly seeing life. Every human being is an undiscovered parallel universe, and no one has time to see everything. To live first means to see, not to define oneself.

Tiresias especially. S/he enters and exits the day-to-day by swimming the breaststroke across great distances, rejecting definitions with Olympian vigour. Of course, not everyone grasps the scope of her/his sexual flickering. Yet Tiresias is convinced that Sandrine is able to read these shifts, his/her transitions from one sex to the other, in contrast to most of her/his colleagues and friends who don't see them.

Sandrine stretches out her arm, slowly mumbles some words that come out of her mouth, grappling with syntax.

Tiresias vacillates quickly between male and female, her/his identity flickers, revealing his/her state just beneath the skin. S/he gently trembles into a doctor, always reverting back to a novice faced with the labour of death. Why has s/he gotten attached to this young patient more than to the others? S/he can't exactly answer this question. For sure, it's commonly known at the centre that an unusual camaraderie exists between her/him and Sandrine. Nothing will keep him/her from watching over Sandrine.

It is six in the evening on Saturday, July 28, 2012.

Sandrine shakes her head, seems agitated, utters a few words with a vindictive force.

—No, Mom, it's no use, it's no use...

Beautiful beyond reproach, things fade one letter at a time. Tiresias stops right in the middle of a male incarnation, takes the young girl's arm, rubs her joints with cautious tenderness. From his pocket, he takes out Joseph

Delteil's *Cholera*, a sort of phantasmagorical novel from the 1920s, with underage nymphs galore in an absurdist and surrealist universe that prefigured Boris Vian. He opens it at random and reads this passage:

> Oh Sun, oh you gobbler of microbes and regenerator of jaundice, killer of Evil and Baptism, you destroy cities, aeroplanes, and women's dresses! Naked and naked, Streams and geometry. No more sixth floors or rotaries. Oh! this irruption of suns in the Augean stables!

Inspired, Tiresias then writes on the back of a hospital form:

> *Sandrine, there is no god, no soul. We all conceal thousands of plants, a hundred thousand stalks that sprout, wither, and die. The self's militant bees often get lost in the melee of our garden. Some forget to pollinate their choices. Our piece of earth turns back into humus with a determination that is always beyond us. You are a trillion cells looking for light, a colony of organic beings struggling to breathe, live, wilt in the fields, and shrivel from use. The sun is the eruption we are destined at the end.*

Suddenly pulling himself together, Tiresias walks around the room, agitatedly rubbing his eyes and temples. Too much moisture in the caruncles. It won't work, he knows it won't work, why does he want to offer some new ritual to this child, an atheist ceremony observing the final hours of her body? He's not sure, goes to the washroom and comes back. Aunt Evelyne has been notified and will be arriving any minute now. He has no choice, he's looking for some significant way to mark the passing of her life and feels deeply ashamed for wishing to dress Sandrine's last agony in his personal mix of poetry and literature that simultaneously evokes the banality and blatant mystery of the world.

Leaning against the wall, s/he purses her/his lips. How many dying children has s/he attended since coming to the centre in 2008? Is s/he trying to sublimate the difficult moments of her/his past? Has something in him/her changed? And why?

All rituals address our foolish questions. We don't have any brilliant answers for a reason to live, and our inner theatre imagines a choreography of loopholes that drug our perceptions. Tiresias is experiencing real suffering and doesn't exactly know how to deal with it. Is it possible to see a hundred children die and remain strangely professional, detached, so formidably clinical that whatever optimal care is possible is provided in each case? S/he has always behaved with the utmost professionalism.

Is s/he betraying the Hippocratic Oath? No. On the contrary, s/he applies it diligently, maintaining the last scraps of life animating her/his patients until the smallest cell involved in making our meaningful identity, our living skeleton, takes its final bow, concedes the work to the bacteria and microorganisms taking over, recolonizing, as the natural conquistadores that they are, the complex fauna of our abandoned body.

Tiresias and the slow migration from medicine to poetry, 2012

Shim Tiresias. August 8, 2012.

"Sandrine's death has cut me to the quick," she keeps telling herself as though she has to find a way to explain her bewilderment.

The images are of an approximated medicine, the luminous dregs supporting the irreproachable life dream. Shim Tiresias has not become cynical or uptight; she analyzes the words fusing under her emotional microscope.

Why this patient and not another? To what do we owe our epiphanies? How much does a person actually weigh in the crucible of our days? What decides that having reached the threshold, attending to another dying child becomes unbearable?

Yet that's what happened. A fence, a border, a communal path was drawn with Sandrine's death. The carapace of knowledge and calm self-denial cracked. A sticky liquid came out. She needed to take a step back—an accepted way of saying that one is standing at the edge of a precipice and must step back to not fall in.

*

Shim Tiresias took a month off work. A month to write,

devote herself to poetry out of spite, shut herself up in her aloofness.

She writes. Attends poetry readings. Gets moved by every little thing, then realizes that she swallows it all, records her experiences of trudging along, focuses on momentary frustrations. How do you treat Sisyphean tyranny? What medicine do you prescribe to those who have stopped accumulating knowledge and begun gathering dust? Shim Tiresias accepts her duplicity. She is wordless, all the while pouring words into her soft skull, the quagmire of her thick head.

Tonight, she's at Dièse Onze, a jazz club located in a nineteenth-century stone cavern that features live music and poetry readings. Arriving just after the opening act, a lineup of young poets participating in the Belle Gueule Poetry Prize—ridiculous prize, quality jury (Nicole Brossard, Kim Doré, Jean-Marc Desgent)—she orders a beer. Another dumbfounded loner is fiddling with his drink, two stools to her left.

Puffy eyes, greasy hair, black cotton shirt revealing his stomach pouch, Daniel (that happens to be his name) turns toward the doctor and, without any introduction, launches into an enthusiastic monologue about one poet's delivery in the first part of the evening. A prose poem, real-life experience, a stint in the hospital that the poet has put into words. Daniel is trying to explain the nuanced emotions he felt while listening to the poet describe the care he had received during his illness. Of course, no one has told him he's talking to a doctor. The coincidence is funny. Shim acts dazed and delighted, she listens. She doesn't want to interrupt him, spoil such a purely confident move. Besides, what exactly would revealing her profession add to the conversation? Establish some facts; comment on certain technical aspects of the story she's swallowing; speak about her experience as a palliative care doctor? No. That would be awkward.

Daniel is right. We should speak. Truthfully or approximately. Without hesitation, we should use our pharynx, glottis, tap our tongue against our palate. Sugar water, speech is nothing more than an exudate of our tension, feeding the air. A sad beauty, speech is simply an offering to another. Shim receives it. She is busy receiving it, professionally. She receives it. With all the patience involved in receiving the filtered water with which we baptize our daily emotions. She receives it. This receptive position pleases her. Hearing the other empty himself of a linguistic impulse reminds her of something a university professor used to say: "A doctor without ears is a fly without wings."

During her residency, she had absorbed grandiose metaphors, sharp, halting condescension, routine sufficiency, syrupy, scholarly arrogance, professional secrets, pat phrases for teaching solutions to the hungry student. But she had particularly relished the incursion into the world of insects to define the physician. Besides, did she really have any more power than an insect in the vast anthill of life? Sure, antibiotics, hygiene, and neonatal care had helped to save young beings who would otherwise have been earth and dust today. But fundamentally, doctors have no impact on general statistics. They can't change the constant ratio between birth and death. Thanks to advances in medicine, we die older and suffer less while alive. It would be stupid to deny this. We must give credit where credit is due. Yet doctors don't save all that much; at best, the greatest scientists do nothing more than simply redirect the labour of death. In fact, doctors save themselves first. They save themselves by taking an overdose of qualifications to overcome their angst.

The ratio is 2.42857142857 births for every death. Being born is always more advantageous for our genes.

Birth is the only brutal violence that is not blameworthy in our right-wing societies (who to blame?). But death, always resourceful, remains the great master of existential angst. If we take away some of its territory on the left, it will seek it on the right. If we eradicate an infectious disease, a new virus will squat in the sector. If we help some North American kids die with dignity, more children will lie strewn on the seedy streets of Khartoum. The insidious effects of the balance between birth and death. From a distance, from high above, from under the dome of a university dedicated to demographics, all this just looks like fluid mechanics.

Daniel finishes his monologue/reportage.

Shim nods her head.

They turn back to their beers, a frank pleasure. A woman, who introduces herself as the host of a literary radio program, announces the start of the second set, featuring readings by Roger des Roches and Louise Dupré.

The sluggish audience, mostly poets who read in the first set and some eccentric diehards who are poetry fans for vague reasons (because they dream of being published by a professional publishing house, or simply because poetry controls their depression, anxiety, or psychosis by offering a remedy worthy of the name that can heal the strange pain of their malaise), politely applauds.

Shim's palms crush the air like a noisy, makeshift pump.

Ninelle, 2007—A few weeks before the last concert

Without movie theatres, atheists wouldn't have any churches.

Ninelle drags Sandrine to the Cineplex Odeon Quartier Latin to see *Ratatouille* by Pixar and Disney. Being six years old, the child doesn't hold back her joy but expresses it with a conviction that is beautiful to watch. She dives into the story, a dark immersion into the narrative, a sequence of flowing images, spiralling characters with elastic gestures stuck in spectacularly realistic scenes, objects, utensils, fruit and cakes, soups and breads bursting through the screen, showing off their appetizing textures. Everything mimes reality so well that blissful amazement becomes the distinctive trait of the emotions the gambist feels in 2007.

—Mom, is the tall man a bad guy?

Looking like Nosferatu, Anton Ego embodies the uncompromising and disdainful critic, petty and elitist. The character appears in the opening shot, to broadcast, in opposition to the opinions of the pot-bellied chef, Auguste Gusteau, that cooking is an art reserved for the great masters. Gusteau counters Ego—akin to democracy versus the aristocracy, access to knowledge versus private education. But viewers understand that the main bad guy in the film is not the one you might think. Pretty soon, they recognize the pecuniary disposition of Chef

Gusteau's successor. A flat face, a pencil-thin moustache, a mean-spirited and battle-ready look will quickly convince the whole movie theatre of his malicious intentions.

—No, the tall man is not really the bad guy, he's just a bit uptight.

Ego is a secondary character; the real star of the film is Remy, a young rat. When he teaches the clumsy Alfredo Linguini how to cook by controlling him like a marionette, pulling his hair to move his arms, a wave of laughter bursts out.

The children are won over.

Sandrine sits with a bag of buttered popcorn next to her mother, who's shivering and gripping her sweater tight in her right fist. No mic is present; we can't hear their conversation. Perhaps they aren't talking; that's likely what's happening. Despite everything, education creeps in. Exposed to an animated film made by a team of progressive intellectuals seeking ways to express their own confusion at being oppressed by the proponents of a money-oriented life, childhood soon ends. Let us be clear, parents and the degree of comfort they offer their offspring is what prolongs childhood, indefinitely or in small doses. Ninelle is strangely optimistic in this regard. A pessimist about everything else, but an optimist in this. Mostly because music keeps her above the fray, both as someone privileged to have received this gift and as someone receptive to the best kind of cerebral massage. The momentum of the notes keeps her at the centre of something important, at the crossroads of taut hope and magical rigour.

Hope is a staple growing in the garden of notes.

Sandrine tastes this artistic assurance. Music doesn't need words; it adheres with more fervour to the reality deep in the brain; it stimulates the neurons and active areas on the scanner more precisely.

The affected and grandstanding critic, a bit like a farmyard administrator, has nevertheless touched Ninelle. It's a cliché to say it, but learning an instrument, whatever degree of raw talent might be involved, remains a gruelling experience. But how can she talk to her daughter about art, yet spare her the lesson about the constant work, the others' indifference, and the overwhelming solitude it demands? Besides, should one talk about art like this with a six-year-old child? No, not yet, she tells herself. It's not yet time for the food mill of guilt and results. Not yet time for the resolute life, eyes fixed on rigour and the siren call of success. Not yet. Not right away. Yet she knows the speed of the current when the will starts imagining future scenarios. But not yet. She resists, counters the rationale of success. Not yet.

Sandrine chews and swallows a handful of phosphorescent yellow popcorn, her lips glistening with butter. Intelligent and mischievous, absorbed by the screen, she doesn't notice her mother wince, hold back a tear of emotion on seeing the spectacle of her daughter's childhood. With her right hand, Ninelle crushes her cardigan, her scraps of bitterness, her dark thoughts. She tells herself that at worst, two years from now, when her daughter is eight, she will tell her about the demands of art.

For now, mother and daughter celebrate beauty without asking why.

Puncto reflexionis

[THE THREE LOVES]

Being good to someone while only pretending to appreciate them (1) is worse than doing them harm while appreciating them (2), which is less optimal than being good to them while also loving them (3).

    Being good while pretending to love = antagonistic love

    Doing harm while loving = inept love

    Being good while loving = ideal love

All life long, we struggle to attain this ideal of being good to someone while loving them. Who would dare to say the opposite without feeling they're failing to keep their most intimate promises? Nevertheless, what we witness, of course, is a subtle combination of the three cases, constantly mixed into the daily soup. Who doesn't ever pretend, and who does everything perfectly? Besides, a surplus of perfection often signifies a surplus of appearances, and an excess of failures indicates either an inability to love oneself, and therefore love others, or a mental defect. We can't get away with it. Curious bystanders, friends, lovers, children look straight into our eyes and assess the temperature of the equilibrium between our intentions and our actions.

Eric and Sandrine, 2005

The bus driver is a stout man in his thirties with a chubby face, sparse chinstrap beard, cheerful eyes. His bus is crowded, the street narrow, bicyclists weave between the cars moving at a snail's pace. We're in Montreal, in a busy neighbourhood.

Eric and Sandrine only just fit at the front of the Nova Bus. Sandrine's father, in good humour, presses his daughter against his hips and stretches his arm to grip the vertical bar next to the driver. Making sure he's balanced, he decides to say a kind word to the anonymous skipper navigating the heavy swell of the streets.

—You need to have eyes in the back of your head to be a bus driver!

Used to people talking to him, the young man doesn't even glance at Eric before saying, without missing a beat:

—I use the same technique with my kids!

"Excellent hand-eye-foot coordination," the qualification for a bus driver according to the guide of specific skills associated with all jobs in existence. "Hand-eye-foot coordination and foreseeing the future," qualifications for becoming an acceptable parent, or at least one who doesn't look like a deflated dinghy in a rushing river.

Eric smiles. He appreciates the repartee.

It is 2005, barely thirteen months before the end of all his expectations.

Sandrine, 2012—Illness + Two years

Jean-Duceppe Park, May 22, 2012.

Two teens followed by two adults, a group of punks, a grandmother dressed in faded colours, and a woman in her fifties with fuzzy hair tied back like a straw hat are walking one after another in a curious procession. Each in turn plays their part in the symphony of others. Each follows the path, the line of desire, that starts at the corner of André-Laurendeau Street, in front of the Emily Dickinson Home.

A day of respite in Sandrine's chronic pain, the afternoon volunteer has received permission to take her to the park. Transporting her is a feat, but once arrived on the lawn of Jean-Duceppe Park, the sick girl savours a few minutes' rest.

A squat man, another taller one, two bespectacled students holding hands, a young girl with her father, a group of teens with heavily made-up faces, and two old guys with sparkling blue eyes, sporting black jackets, a banner, and intimidating vigour, march past on the same path. Sandrine watches this surprising, colourful procession. Speechless, she examines the flow of things, life's constant disobedience, all these people defying a government already overtaken by public opinion for many weeks now. Bill 78 was passed on May 18. People are still in the streets on May 22.

69

At times the heart of a people, the social body, reacts with force to the raging metastases of chaotic power, which is corrupted at the source and perpetuates the subtle oligarchy we still call "democracy."

In school, they teach us two essential things: life is an outstanding debt to settle and a responsibility to assume with as much conviction as possible. Obligations and debts are the two faces of our privilege-granting society. Privileges are accorded to those who no longer have any particular obligations or crippling debts, and for the rest, the obligations and debts just keep piling up. As connecting vessels, obligations and debts are self-regulating.

Sandrine doesn't dare say out loud what she secretly thinks inside. The volunteer then offers her thoughts, vaguely addressing her protege.

—I think this movement is great. All these people saying they've had enough.

The people keep marching in the same direction, convinced of their newly found obligation, an obligation now confined to simply saying what they think, in the street, without suit jackets, decrees, rulings, and legal letters composed by swindlers of the status quo. The people march with their scraps of imperfection, their square patches of hope, their petty grievances and wishes pinned to black-and-red flags. The people march, awkwardly or with agility, in shirts of hardship and blouses of injustice, hungry for something rare.

Sandrine thinks of her mother, still alive but disconnected from the flow, out of tune. Why do they criticize her for no longer being responsible, for no longer having debts? She is now parked in an anteroom, like her daughter. Dumping grounds of frozen memories, plastic bracelets with file numbers on their wrists, they are two fallow humans with no harvest on the horizon. Two humans waiting for the fermata and final bar line marking the end of everyone's score.

On her sweater, Sandrine Berthiaume-Côté has pinned what one must pin to be part of the movement. The volunteer is pinning the red square—a scrap of felt cut out during a workshop with the residents of the Emily Dickinson Home—to her own T-shirt. Everyone now wears solidarity on their chests in this small beacon of life's ambiguous purpose.

Everyone wears their pride on their torsos, cardigans, T-shirts, blouses, cut with four snips of the scissors.

Tiresias, 2012—Sexual flickering/Advent of the prayer wave

Tiresias is listening to a recording of Sandrine's mother.

A member of the Studio de musique ancienne de Montréal, Ninelle had recorded a few CDs at a time when distribution among the small community of early music fans was still viable. Music streaming would soon prevail, flattening out diversity by mechanically imposing it—as a current pharmacopoeia that hiccups, laps, and rejoices—without too many transitions for us to appreciate stasis.

Mid-water, with a flat left breast and a swollen right breast, Tiresias jots down the lyrics of a part s/he remembers.

> Prayer is an endless chain of purest love
> Whose active virtue is described:
> It pulls divinest graces from above.
> It linketh us to God, and God to us.

Composed by John Ward, this Protestant verse anthem celebrates the unfailing relay of prayer as a means of getting closer to God. The work evokes the infinite cycle of the will, innocently presaging Schopenhauer's intuition three centuries later.

It is the advent of the prayer wave, a radio message, a digital signal broadcast into space in search of the absolute receiver. A strange foreshadowing of satellites, radio, short wave, and fibre optics.

Protestantism had one advantage over Catholicism: it liberated believers from the yoke of other earthly power, from other secular domination over their behaviour. Persecutions and dogmatism continued out of decorum, as much against the body as was possible, but a chain had been established, a direct call to God advocated, in the most perfect cacophony of the epoch.

Penis almost gone, testicles retracted, mammary protuberances established, Tiresias walks around her condo, smelling the increasingly prominent aroma of the Old-Fashioned Pea Soup simmering in his kitchen. An assortment of fragrances, a sweet and salty bouquet combined with the fatty scent of peas now liquefied and releasing their milk, the soup (whose recipe s/he nabbed from Ricardo's website) embalms the apartment with its traditional perfume. S/he always feels the same enthusiasm when the beans, of mineral hardness, after being soaked for several hours and boiled for two, release their juices and transform the clear broth into a caloric brew of rare density.

Tiresias dips the ladle into the thick, bubbling substance. With a full bowl, s/he walks to the living room. Sits on the faux-leather armchair with its side lamp and stirs the surface and depth of the bowl. Steam dances around hir hand holding the burning-hot contents. S/he glances at the library shelves while the silky, greasy substance flows down hir esophagus. Grabs Joseph Delteil's *Cholera*, pleased to discover this book among hir paraphernalia of old novels with yellowed spines. Curious, s/he leafs through the pages, reads the first line:

I was born on December 25 at midnight, to a muzhik and a great duke.

S/he continues to devour hir evening meal while holding the book taken out of its box of oblivion in one hand. S/he wants something really wild to inspire hir.

It's no small thing to watch over a child's imminent death. You have to balance on history's branches, compile works, and invent rituals on a daily basis, mimicking the scales of ordinary madness.

The idea is to keep surprising the young patient without frightening her, offer her the best finish by planing like a patient cabinetmaker the piece of furniture that will welcome her self-cocoon, her siren of being-with, the last siren to sound before matter becomes frivolous and metamorphoses.

Tiresias's breasts dilate, retract, disappear, and reappear.

Tomorrow, s/he will read Sandrine a text inspired by *Cholera* as an atheist anthem to death. Convinced by some tenuous link between her mother's records, the startling surrealism of Delteil (who became a mystical writer a few years later), and hir intention to no longer read flavourless, idiotic, or moral texts to accompany the trial of death.

Sandrine's five-year birthday, 2006

The Obelix-shaped piñata hangs in the Berthiaume-Côté living room.

Children circle the prey with a broomstick, hitting the package of candy with waning vigour.

—Is it working, Dad?

—Try it like this!

The father lifts up his daughter, aims the mini-jet of her force at the helmeted head of hair. The children shriek, scream, something's happening, a meagre obstacle to candy demands an excess of violence from their small hands. But it's no use. At most, Sandrine combs and smooths the big guy's hair with the broom handle. The contents remain inaccessible. A poor, cheap mystery that stimulates everyone's aggression. The adults hesitate, wait patiently, treat the situation objectively at first, then, like an increasing curve that suddenly rises exponentially, they change course, start screaming too, struggling with their commonplace greed. It all happens so quickly that the preprogrammed response of their febrile cells doesn't worry anyone for three seconds, until Jordan's dad lets loose a stupid directive.

—We're not gonna make it easy for them!

It is at this moment that Eric, until now preoccupied with supporting his daughter's attempts at destruction, secretly recalls the anxiety-provoking film he once saw

77

on CBC in his youth. The story is about a couple in their thirties who row to an Italian or South American island—he can't remember—where all the adults have vanished. Freud's *unheimlich* seeps through the heavy silence. The camera follows the couple, closely framing their exploration of the deserted streets. Everything is still, riddled with absent noises. Then a child quickly crosses an intersection. Drawn by the movement, the woman wonders who the runner is. The man decides to walk in the direction the boy has gone. Indistinct giggles of children can be heard beyond the walls. Surprised by the pulsating clamour on the other side of a double door, the couple stops in front of it. Through a small square opening, they can hear the din of children's voices goading one of their own into an unknown task. Uneasy, the woman cautiously pushes the small wooden partition. The camera then dives into an immense room, the sound goes up several decibels, and, at first, we see a billhook attached to the end of a pole waving about in the air. Then the camera zooms in on the face of a poor, terrified woman in a skirt, tied up and hanging from the ceiling on a meat hook. The viewer understands at the same time as the couple that the bound and horrified woman swinging on the end of a rope is in fact a live piñata.

The children continue to shout altogether, the camera points to the floor, and we realize the pole with the billhook is being wielded by a blindfolded young girl who is blindly striking the air, trying to sink the sharp edge of her tool into the body of the gagged, writhing, imploring woman/piñata. The image turns to the petrified eyes of the woman in the couple witnessing the scene, zooming in on her pupils.

Silence returns. The couple flees. The chase begins. The horror can continue.

Three seconds of these fleeting images are enough to produce harsh feelings in Eric. Eager to put an end to this suddenly evil-seeming piñata, he grabs the stick in his daughter's hands, holding it lower down on the handle, and gives a sudden, sharp whack to the stomach of the simple-minded-looking Obelix. The body bursts. All the children get splattered with paper. The contents flow out in a cascade of candy wrappers. Sandrine raises her arms in a sign of victory. Her father sets her down amidst the frenzy. Like all her friends, she throws herself on the tumulus of candy, a ridiculous homage to the fake suffering of a human effigy.

The tension drops.

They've just transformed a blood ritual into children's treats.

Tiresias, 2012—*Puncto reflexionis*
[THE SCRIPT MAKES US ALL CRAZY]

No one asks us to approve the script. No one introduces us to the main actors. Yet everyone goes into it with joy in their eyes, moist lips, and feeling good-natured at heart.

If we stop to think about it, this is what we're given.

Whatever anyone might say, to educate means instilling doubt about the viability of the original script. At the end of the day, we are given a thousand much more scintillating parts than ours in other parallel films, and we are told: "Aspire to this, desire this rather than your sorry-ass life."

Surprisingly, bitterness or discontent should be what shapes our channels to others. We should all be breaking windows, shaking up the established order, and bashing the lesson-givers. But why is it that everything is curbed, lined with warm fleece, subdued by the natural span of the living environment? Why is it that only a small fraction of people bang the can, speak out against hidden injustice, and cry for the dismissal of the scriptwriter?

For Tiresias, it has been an odious mystery since elementary school. Odious because outrageously incomprehensible: a mystery that sticks to the bottom of the pan and can't be dislodged.

Why was it that he barely studied, yet received almost perfect marks, while some of his friends reviewed their notes a thousand times and struggled to work their way a few points above average?

He hadn't voted for this disparity, but he recognized it. Some of his classmates from the top of the pile, after a few years of academic domination, also developed the affected, mannered, and detached attitude of those "doomed to cram for their basic needs," an attitude associated with the only persisting aristocracy still tolerated in our so-called Republican or Democratic world, the aristocracy of the intelligentsia (which is not entirely correct either, since the aristocracy of wealth has the power to accept any old dunce to the school of privilege). A kind of added value of the mind promises those most on the ball a future free of money worries, an almost infinite guarantee of comfort, property, and travel. The mechanics of privilege channels money upward without restraint, while a few raffles and lotteries redistribute sometimes significant amounts to the masses and make people like the Lavigueur family multimillionaires (we'll skip over the tragic outcome of that story).

In Tiresias's circle of informed, intelligent friends, abreast of the economic and scientific studies consulted by the decision-makers, no one gets overly worked up, they set the record straight (a way of remembering the rationale—which, after all, is not that unjust—of this peculiar system in which they have gained their important roles), they balance it out with some soul-searching. His friend Étienne Ducroux is not the only one to belabour the point of "no one dies of hunger in Quebec, it's impossible, there's a relief organization to address each of our flaws."

True, Quebec is not a disaster zone, and most people who hold down two minimum-wage jobs or manage to budget their meagre earnings (less than $18,000 per year) don't clog up the emergency rooms and soup kitchens. Though some go to the emergency for minor ailments, which makes them seem demanding and detestable in the eyes of the decision-makers and alarmists, but as soon as they develop a major kidney problem, break a leg, or have a heart attack, modern medicine welcomes them with open arms and without making a fuss, providing quality care free of charge, as long as they have an official or illegal health insurance card.

But living doesn't just mean surviving and cheating death a few times, aided by a social machine that pulls one from the clutches of illness. No. Living means being able to get out of the cycle of loneliness, boredom, and expectations, having carefree access to new pleasures and no money worries.

We're not quite there yet, even if we should never again complain on a full stomach, as his privileged friends tell him, in our decent province that stands well above the pack. A reasoning tempered by complacency. There is nothing magical about the original script, and those who take themselves for social magicians have no convincing cure-all to offer for our most common anxieties. Social inequalities persist, but in a context where the grimy, ragged, sooty poverty of Charles Dickens is a thing of the past. The social paradigms have changed, but granting favours to the rich while asking average citizens to tighten their belts—the "Bernie Ecclestone" effect, he being a seeker of government aid for the Montreal Grand Prix—

among other things, illustrates the socially unjust slap that we still unapologetically give people.

Standing on the sidewalk, Tiresias ruminates.

*

A tireless walker, strolling in the city and rambling through neighbourhoods, Tiresias stops in front of the Centre du Plateau at 2275 Saint-Joseph East. Now an office and family-based community centre, this building reminds him of his adolescence in the 1980s. The facade, an abstract pediment hanging above the entrance, features a bas-relief reminiscent of Calder's mobiles or Henry Moore's large sculptures. Five circular forms drawn in a naive line (the Communist aesthetic of the 1960s) fit together like the Olympic rings. On the ground, between the entrance and the street, these same characters are repackaged in a sculpture in the round. Each head forms the pistil of a unique flower or a flame flickering in an imagined breeze.

Basically, characters who dance.

Somewhat like Tiresias in 1984, in the basement of this building, at the time a large gymnasium with blue and red lines, metal anchors for badminton nets, and cinder-block walls covered in a thick layer of cream paint. An era of spaghetti-strap purses, thrown on the floor in the middle of the dancers, everyone shaking to the quick snare taps of Rod Stewart or Kool & the Gang, keeping their spot around the future active uteruses. This ritual secretly celebrated the recognized fertility of the young women in his group, now sexually active. Tiresias, who

84

didn't sexually flicker in 1984, remembers the gendered insouciance, the wall of certainty that comforted him in his sensual agitation around the leather, cotton, synthetic uteruses, collapsed, extended, strewn across the gymnasium floor. A kind of Louise Bourgeois sculpture, a reflection of the absolute.

The absolute of "Tonight I'm Yours" and "Get Down on It."

> I say people, what? What you gonna do?
> You've gotta get on the groove
> If you want your body to move, tell me, baby

The command of the moving body, of the body destined to party and fuck—a "take it or leave it" ideology asserting the invigorating greatness of no tomorrow—the command of the grind and bang of night, of the contrast between the sexes on display. Life as a continual, open exploitation of the other, without expectations, without hindsight, without the tyranny of good and evil, an aimless breathlessness in the beneficial void that ostracizes and produces goods. It was something like that.

To guide it all, dogmatic handclaps wove a Frost fence between the explosive chorus and the funk glissandi of "Just an Illusion."

> Searching for a destiny that's mine
> There's another place another time
> Touching many hearts along the way yeah
> Hoping that I'll never have to say
> It's just an illusion, illusion, illusion

The volcano of others is just some extra noise, a reverberation of life's ennui. The volcano of others erupts at any moment, piercing the overly blue sky with diffracted rays. The volcano of others is the main illusion that makes it possible for us to keep hoping.

With a curiosity as natural as his convoluted conclusions, and fascinated by the volcano metaphor, Tiresias imagines other phrases to describe his fleeting thoughts, starts transforming into a woman again, this time with the slowness of the academician, round testicles shrinking with clumsy insistence between her buttocks as she sits on a wet patch of Coca-Cola. The black ice of park benches, the Coke seeps through fabric like the eternal, invisible glue of an indistinct, urban puddle. Shim tries to wipe her behind but only manages to spread the caramelized substance on her fingers.

Everything that sticks is multiform, s/he tells hirself.

Everything that sticks resembles a perfect illusion.

The columbarium, 2004

Eric Berthiaume learned the meaning of *columbarium* in 2004. It was in a song by Pierre Lapointe, a gypsy rhythm with lyrics dipped in irony. He liked the song but wondered what it was about.

Realizing our ignorance reminds us that we are born from want and we live in want.

—It's a place for storing funeral urns.

His musician lover knew more about the subject than him.

Actually, Lapointe's lyrics intrigued them both. The image of "licking the panes of the columbarium" left them dumbfounded. But it was poetry, Ninelle decided, and highlighting the consumerist, voyeuristic aspect of those who frequent columbaria—these Costcos of memories, these shelves of ashes—in itself made sense.

To continue this conversation in the car, while Sandrine, strapped in her child seat, was crying capriciously, proved to be impossible.

Exit Lapointe.

Play Mom and Dad's greatest hits of comfort.

Tiresias, 2008—The early days in pediatric palliative care

For the remains of your beloved little one. Different sizes according to the age of the child. There's a whole industry, with a wide range of choice. In porcelain, in marble, in cherry wood, in crystal. In all kinds of shapes: teddy bears, rabbits, little pink or blue shoes, little trucks, dolls with heads you can unscrew, seagulls flying off. The business of death is inevitably kitsch. Maybe kitsch is soothing.[1]

Kitsch is always soothing. Tiresias was sure of it. Kitsch is soothing because it helps us to oppose the commonplace (despised by snobs) or to confirm our mental images (reassure tacky people). In both cases, it works.

A doctor faced with broken-down parents. A doctor transformed into an answer terminal for human beings deprogrammed by grief over their child, Tiresias had an arsenal of "process" reading materials for the battered.

Tom Is Dead by Marie Darrieussecq held a prime spot in hir repertoire. The novel is about a mother mourning the death of her four-and-a-half-year-old son. The writer touches on various aspects related to this ordeal and tells the story in a fragmented style, very effective for providing

---

1. Marie Darrieussecq, *Tom Is Dead*, trans. Lia Hills (Melbourne: Text Publishing, 2009), 66.

nuances, enumerating fleeting experiences, or revealing the thought process and showing suffering. Mourning a child is a microcosm in itself, a country invented by pain. Getting out requires exploring this terrain as well as becoming aware of the distance separating us from its borders.

Because the mother's carefree attitude created the context that led to Tom's accidental death, she tosses and turns in a vortex of guilt. In a passage in which the main character, Darrieussecq's alter ego (since the novel is written like an autobiography[2]), realizes that the mother of a young girl who has died of cancer is in a better psychological state than her, she understands something about the logic of mourning. Her grief is clearly more trying than that of the other woman in her support group. Witnessing a body's decline over an entire year spreads the incomprehension over a longer period. It is therefore less painful to acclimatize to it.

Tiresias has offered this book to the tearful families at the Emily Dickinson Home many times. It was when he started working there in 2008 that he had the presence of mind to suggest this title, for the first time, as psychological support after a child's death.

His first patient presented him with a double exception, that of the illness and of a marginalized family. Birmingham Jouvet had an outlandish name and eccentric parents. He was the progeny of garrulous wanderers,

2. Never mind Camille Laurin's accusation of "psychological plagiarism." Every author has the right to be inspired by anyone. One doesn't need to personally experience something to write about it. We are all "literary kleptomaniacs," as Sarah Kane points out in her play *4.48 Psychosis*.

a university couple who had named their son after the city where they had met. A revered place, its memory forever inscribed in their only child's first name. A child they had pampered, a child who was respectful and bright, who had the sharply defined profile of a vessel, a sculpted bow, and whose future Tiresias was sure had looked bright.

It's not grace, as Saint Augustine understood, but rather an evident, cheerful ease bursting with effervescent energy that patches up anything from a minor wound to the most daunting decline. Someone who always pulls through and, by pulling through, pulls fate along with them, drags luck in their wake and sows their story with successes. The death of Birmingham Jouvet at age thirteen was therefore all the stranger. The only way he managed to get rid of the illness he'd endured for two long years of professional palpations and drastic remedies was to run away from it. Do a front somersault as a last resort before immediately diving into what comes after suffering.

With breasts like an eighteenth-century shepherdess, Tiresias had concluded the young boy's odyssey by stroking his hair. Heart throbbing arrhythmically in his temples like a ratchet brace. The doctor hadn't been able to hide her attachment. Two years spent bombarding the deterioration, deploying a thousand tactics to keep the walls standing. Two years spent calming the eruptions of despair from the youth with the cracking voice, scraping the wretched regrowth, protecting the remains of the body's blooms migrating in large numbers toward nothingness. It wears you down. Gets on your nerves. Holds your head underwater.

Instead of crying, since her mucous membranes had a strange mania for damming up, Tiresias made do with what remained. The boy's hair had resisted, had kept its silken texture. A part of the cellular battle that had overcome the impossible, mundane matter brandishing life until the very end. Birmingham's hair was life's victory.

*

They invited him to the funeral service. He showed up anonymously, without ceremony. Out of a sense of decency, he simply nodded. Making a face at the same time. A subtle grimace that expresses sorrow and solidarity all at once. Difficult to describe or name, twenty specific muscles all moving in the same instant. He lived his emotions in private. In public, he had the courteousness of a pachyderm.

As people slowly began migrating toward the buffet, he took the opportunity to approach the urn. The tip of his beard pointed at the object with the incredulity of a novice gambler watching a nag win a race. Faced with the container's originality, some people held back a smile, others unease. After all, the dead have a right to eccentricity. He simply gauged the situation as highly theatrical.

In front of him stood the porcelain head of Philip K. Dick, divided into two sections. The cranium had a large slit in the forehead, separating from the urn to form a lid. The ashes of Birmingham Jouvet rested in the head of Philip K. Dick.

By repeating this phrase mechanically, to convince

himself of what he was seeing, he couldn't suppress a smile.

The ashes of Birmingham Jouvet rested in the head of Philip K. Dick.

Eric, 2006—A few weeks before his death

No nominations for the Gemini Awards this year.

Eric is nonplussed.

No melodrama, not even a concern.

His literary show, basic, lacking an enticing formula—a writer, a word labourer, a capable and sober host who sticks to the essentials, and a director who has no impulse to make a work of art, putting it all together at a good pace—has nothing to seduce those seeking the new. The stars are the books and those who wrote them. He could have given in to the lure of mockery, invited some more mainstream writers, namely those who would please an ignorant and hostile programming committee stuck with the impression that the show is elitist, while knowing he'd only be flogging a dead horse by compromising. Sooner or later, they would cancel the show, bootlicking or not. It's still in production in the summer of 2006; he's content with his situation but knows it won't last. It will be decided in December. Every December sees the return of his anxiety over whether the show will be renewed, something difficult to explain to others.

Those on the outside envy him somewhat. Even Ninelle, who knows her partner's salary provides for the family's immediate needs, avoids talking about money. She teaches a workshop or two now and then, receives grants sometimes, but enjoys the moral and monetary support that the salary of a professional TV researcher provides.

The previous year, two friendly producers, the only tireless allies of these literary minutes on a community channel, had the idea of submitting him and the host to the Geminis. A kind of secondary award held at the end of the year to determine which TV programs and personalities are most appreciated. It would be a lie to say he hadn't felt some pride.

Winning a Gemini doesn't give you many real dividends, other than walking on the red carpet, rubbing shoulders with MC Gilles, suffering his rebellious or grovelling collusion, and adding a line to your CV. A nomination also feeds the false hope that the contracts will magically multiply.

Public opinion exerts an insidious pressure to transform all those who have reached this stage in their career into trendy icons. Having captured the volatile and unforgiving interest of stakeholders, a handful of TV celebrities who have been in the public eye for years produce most of the sympathetic capital generated by the virtual machine. Respect in the milieu and the public's sympathy come at this price: the tyranny of trends. Most mainstream artists comply with the dictatorship of public opinion, afraid of losing their status or having their careers fall apart.

Living from contract to contract means living in the unknown. Living in the unknown means hanging off a cliff, whatever the cost, without paying any attention to the colour or shape of the hook.

Nothing is more brutal yet also more exciting than a career in television. Ratings that hardly waver, invented or real minor sex scandals, opinions that anger people on social media, rumours, programming committee and executive board undermined by a weak cultural vision, new management that wants to hire its proteges and end careers that seem beyond reproach. The history of television in Quebec looks like symbolic trench warfare with no holds barred. Talent, intelligence, luck, no luck, stupidity, constant sublime humour continues, however, to generate excellent programs and encourage those motivated by work well done to accomplish miracles in this cyclone of uncertainty.

Eric has nothing to worry about, however. He's only a researcher. Free to be anything since he doesn't appear onscreen. His main tasks include running around in the wings and on the set, doing any relevant research, writing and printing out the documents that his dear host (the first to believe in him) awaits to prepare his interviews, contacting writers and celebrities. A researcher is a copy editor, a writer, a press officer, and an email or telephone pest. He's there to ensure that the invited guests arrive on set at the appointed time and that they sign a release form, a cursory document attesting to the use of their image. The image that will enter the lives of thousands of people. Nothing less than thousands of people in television, even community TV.

He doesn't really understand the barely disguised snobbery of mainstream artists discreetly mocking the ratings of shows on Télé-Québec or cable networks. The employees of his community channel have a stock response to this disregard for numbers: "Filling up the Bell Centre every week—that's a lot of people, no?"

Forty thousand people doesn't count for much in the milieu; it's residual, feeble, laughable as a viewership. Three times this number would be enough to catch the eye of a mainstream host who lives only for the ratings. We can already picture him admitting to the commercial failure of his television project on a popular late-night show hosted by France Beaudoin (over 400,000 viewers). You're marked for life if one day you become part of the millions club. The camera would catch you sympathizing on the air; you'd make some fatalistic generalizations about the challenges of creating a successful program or about the impenetrable mystery of shows that get a million viewers. The cameraperson on four would capture two or three micro-grimaces of pain on your dramatically crestfallen face. That would be plenty. The compassion of spectacle doesn't ask for more.

Besides, no one would take the time to philosophize about the importance of the number. One hundred and twenty thousand people watching the same channel at the same time. One hundred and twenty thousand. Twice the capacity of the Olympic Stadium.

There is something indecent about the unrecognized influence of so many individuals. Below 400,000, the sponsors remain lukewarm and the advertisers cautious. At twenty or forty thousand per show, the team takes on the role of blue-collar television workers, programming fillers, the small fry on the air.

When the show first aired, the reviews were good and the public followed suit. The host, well-known in the cultural milieu, would often be stopped on the street by viewers satisfied with his work and the content of the show. Popular with the public, popular with the producers who had created it, good-natured atmosphere on the set, director happy to be filming, technicians chummy with the writers and host, everything seemed to predict a few more years of this show about books.

Without being naive, Eric hopes that things will move forward.

In a way, he will slip out of his life at a moment when everything is balanced. During one of the flat stages when everything corresponds to an optimal state of the humble joys demanded of life: no money worries, loving girlfriend, bright child, constant joie de vivre, familial micro-community in good health, his lover's career flourishing, rewarding work in an environment he cherishes.

He is perched on a hillock of tranquility.

Clear-headed, he remains cautious, on guard against bouts of happiness, but he doesn't hold back from taking advantage and enjoying life, like anyone else who, after going up a long incline, ends up in a sunny clearing.

No. This year, no nominations for the Gemini.

When he first started out, he even forgot that his show was eligible for such an award. He didn't think about it. The etiquette made him laugh. The TV gala rather bored him. He didn't feel in competition with his colleagues. Besides, he couldn't stand pettiness and stayed moderate. But ever since participation in the Gemini quarterfinals became possible, he hasn't had a choice, he has learned to want more, it's human nature, and in this respect, he's disappointed and secretly saddened. It's barely a muffled honk on his future road. A fly darting into his field of vision, nothing to declare or verbalize in daily conversation.

A trivial irritation that, though he doesn't know it yet, he'll never share with his family. Just as he'll never hear the bad news that his show will be cancelled a few months later. Pressure from the CRTC regarding the channel's community mandate, run-ins with lawyers, vendettas against the channel's proprietary syndicate, complicated battles happening several floors above his workplace will finally get the better of this small mercy, a brief respite between two media crises and administrative clashes.

The artisans of television are either very lucky or very screwed. He will die lucky.

This summer, on Route 116 toward Richmond, he will lose the faculty of making something out of nothing.

Josiane, 2011—Follow-up & end

People who know what they want are rare.

Willpower is always an out-of-place element hovering over our lives, worse than thick smoke. We reap its debris like acid rain.

Josiane sips her tea in the pale morning air. Today she's going back to Sandrine. She doesn't really know how to approach her second attempt at being charming and playful. The hot liquid moistens her lips, and her eyes, staring at the rim of the cup, seem dazed.

Between her two kinds of ideas, the bad ones she's had and those to come, the only thing that matters at the moment is her ritual of reflection. Her library, a hodgepodge of shelves holding a phenomenal number of books in the calmest clutter, offers an accurate portrait of her jumbled-up thoughts. Not because the student suffers from confusion, but rather from mental stagnation. An internal rumble that goes nowhere, brief ruminations from which clear ideas struggle to extricate themselves.

The only remedy is movement. Walking, moving through space, feeling the ground under one's feet, emptying one's mind. Half the success gurus out there plainly tell us over and over again: the more we want something, the less we stand to get it. The other half tell us the opposite: the more we want something, the more we stand to get it. One must attain a strange balance between one's desires and how one satisfies them.

Josiane's hands graze the walls of her apartment, a useless but reassuring gesture. She examines her space, attentive to details. *Improvisation* seems to be the key word to remember here.

*

Standing at the top of the stairs, at the front door of the only participant in her art workshop, Josiane doesn't ring the bell yet. She hears a persistent murmur, music bouncing off the wooden walls all the way to the entrance.

Sandrine is singing by herself in a loud voice.

Ringing the bell now feels wrong. Knocking on the glass surface of the door seems best. But Josiane hesitates. She doesn't know if she should interrupt this solitary carnival. The last bastion of daily release, the freedom of "singing my whole presence to the universe." She hears the words distinctly, and her ears gradually decode the syllables: "What's this? What's this?" Staccato rhythm, childish theme, lively words. "What's this? I can't believe my eyes!" A sort of hymn, an invigorating song, with full orchestral arrangement. A musical? The melody sounds familiar, but she can't quite put her finger on its name. Her curiosity is piqued. She wants to know more about this private celebration.

Bam bam bam bam.

Bam bam. (*bis*)

The song continues, Sandrine sings a bit off-key, her

strained vocal cords let a deep emotion escape from her throat.

Bam bam bam bam.

Bam bam. (*bis*)

The volume is turned off.

Josiane is ill at ease. Has she caused an irreversible coolness? Her heart turns a thousand somersaults. Sandrine opens the door with a mischievous smile.

—Want to sing "What's This?" from *The Nightmare Before Christmas* with me?

A spontaneous choreography instinctively takes shape.

*

Running in circles, pressing their eyes to binoculars, growing taller, then instantly shrinking, rolling in pretend snow in the living room, aiming unexpected arrows at objects, miming climbing up a ladder, stirring a dish for the fun of it, playing being owls with their heads, and dancing, dancing, running in circles, pushing the limits of their thoraxes, shaking their arms in make-believe confusion, waving their hands around their heads as though responding to something unspeakable, walking backwards then dashing frantically ahead, pretending to slide on the living room sofa transformed into a snowy slope, laughing for no reason, carefully pinning questions to the calendar, tapping invisible windows with the back of the hands, staring wide-eyed like Mr. Jack, astounded, animated, aghast, waddling about, coming out of a tree whose bark is a unique door, falling to the floor with arms held stiff, staring at the ceiling, clapping hands to the beat of the music, running in circles, dancing, dancing, seeing Sandrine lose consciousness...

Ninelle, 2011—Her Québec exercise book, her great delusion

Note in a Hilroy Québec exercise notebook, left on the night table of patient Ninelle Côté, after her first suicide attempt.

I was born last and I'll die first.

I'm a viper with toad blood, a diet of disease, hemlock cider, devoured. I no longer exist, tell me I'm alive, tell me I understand, tell me I'm not one of Bluebeard's wives buried alive. Dead, I lie in the arms of nothingness. But it's not me, I'm a frozen stretch of road, a pile of rocks, my head thinks with the future, and the future tells me I'm dead. Not animated, frozen in time, with butcher's hooks piercing my cheek, fished by an enthusiast on a lake in northern Denmark.

I'm fully in Mayhem's "Psywar."

My name has escaped, my letters and music discarded. My key has no note, gives no talk on vanity in baroque music, opens only one door: the credo that passes by too quickly for us to catch it. I write because I don't know what else to do, a leech with no veins, depleted. Mist over grass, I exist only in the morning, moistened by accident.

Before, nothing.

During, emptiness.
After, nothing.

Being committed today is rare. Most independent schizophrenics and the marginally insane go about their business as best as they can, integrating themselves into society, thanks to a plethora of associations and shelters. A schizophrenic mother has even published a book explaining how she became a mother by subduing her internal voices.

Mental illness doesn't mean losing one's bearings. It means not giving a damn about finding them.

To merit a room in an institution now, a person has to commit a crazy act of staggering violence. An absolute split from shared experience and mainstream reality coupled with a recognized aggression or self-destructive pathology. Without these clearly identified elements, we let the neurotics, the worriers, the petrified make do with their partial autonomy.

Besides, who can actually claim to be fully autonomous?

We are all partially engaged in a socialization process that initiates us, manages us, defines us.

The truly insane are those who incessantly repeat that they are the makers of their own selves. The truly insane are those who spit out at any moment: "I don't need anyone."

Sandrine's mother suffers from Cotard's syndrome, a serious mental disorder that stages delusions of decay, organ putrefaction, the violent vivisection of the body, gives one the feeling of being dead, the tissues glacially cold. A strange validation of the concept of a non-existent self, the decaying of the body's substance, a dissociative disorder of the highest degree.

In 2011, she still lingered in the hallways of the Douglas institute. Scrawny, scribbling now and then, playing the same three pieces over and over on the old upright piano chained to the wall of the recreation room. The third movement of Fauré's *Pelléas et Mélisande*—the quiet "Sicilienne"—Nina Simone's "Strange Fruit," and Couperin's "Les barricades mystérieuses."

Tiresias, 2012—The story of Carson McCullers

Shim pops the DVD into the external DVD drive of hir
computer.

Sandrine is quiet.

January 2012.

From the very beginning of *The Heart Is a Lonely Hunter*,
the soundtrack of the opening credits—a childlike, inno-
cent melody in the style of Morricone—distils the necessary melancholic syrup. An earworm composed by David
Grusin and played on the harpsichord, this quasi nursery
rhyme sets the film's tone. We're about to enter Carson
McCullers's universe of emotional solitude and sexual
awakening.

For a few hours, the young patient has been hanker-
ing for a movie, any movie, to forget the dismal temperature, rain, freezing ice, slush, sky stuck in the rinse cycle.
Shim dipped into the centre's video library, supplied by
hir own purchases for the most part. Hir medical practice had reaffirmed the fact that in palliative care, culture
constitutes the least harmful and most effective remedy
against our obligation to withstand the hammers of time.
These rhythmic drummers, coxswains of the Roman gal-
leys, remind the body to row, function, whatever the cost,
defying the extraordinary obstacles dragging the boat toward the bottom.

In the collection of films for sensitive young girls,

Tiresias considers *The Heart Is a Lonely Hunter* a classic. Besides informing them about a major American literary work of the twentieth century, a critical and popular success that propelled the twenty-three-year-old author, Carson McCullers, to the forefront of the literary scene, the film addresses a subject relevant to adolescents: sexual awakening. The novel presents the development of a tender relationship between a teenage girl and a deaf-mute man renting a room in her parents' house. Budding feelings, emotional development, and initiation into the adult world are the themes explored.

Sandrine has been raised more or less by this art and its kindness, frightened by its violence, educated by its historical films; she cherishes the cinema. She also reads, but spends more time with moving images, with cinematic, television, or YouTube stories.

For Tiresias, a film never adds up to a simple representation of passive entertainment. Shim sees all the dramatic motivations, settings, characters, subject matter, music, costumes, actors' performances as potential material for development, ideas for workshops, or pretexts for brief catharsis. In this case, the doctor is counting on the fascination exerted by sign language, used by the characters of J. Singer and his pal, Antonapoulos, to get Sandrine interested in this art. Hir goal: show her three or four ways of expressing affection or anger using the words/gestures of such a language. Not to mention that the film's tragic ending will draw forth some beneficial emotions, pull some inhibited existential questions out of the drawer.

To entertain, amuse, and at the same time develop a

sincere camaraderie with hir patients is what interests Tiresias. Locking away sorrows in a lead trunk is pointless. Evoking the prospect of death makes sense—talking about it a little, if only through gestural signs, a choreographed anger interpreted by hands, in order to obtain some temporary respite, momentary relief, in the face of our laughable fate.

Only by visiting the house of pain and screams can we tame our pathetic end, our final exit from the stage. For adults and children alike, messing around with expiry dates is not the best solution.

Sandrine talks about everything and doesn't hold back from asking Tiresias embarrassing questions. Shim feels that s/he needs to respect this healthy curiosity. Especially since s/he cries silently every time s/he watches this film, moved by the strange presence of goodness, the angelic gentleness of the character brilliantly played by Alan Arkin. The deaf-mute's name is "Singer." He represents a redemptive, generous figure who doesn't receive any affection but gives and encourages it everywhere he goes. A buffer spirit, a link to the living, a facilitator of love who will never recover from the death of his slightly mentally disabled friend.

By playing with the buried remains of grief from her own childhood, McCullers was able to create a sensitive masterpiece, a hymn to the heart's solitude, its uncompromising logic.

Heart of gold or heart of mud, everyone dies without having found what they were truly looking for.

Tiresias smiles.

Sandrine is captivated.

For two hours, life looks like something other than catheters, wheelchairs, the smell of hand sanitizer, and the Montreal weather in winter.

Tiresias the music-lover, 2001—*Tenebrae Lessons*

November 2001. *First Tenebrae Lesson.*

Incipit Lamentatio Jeremiae Prophetae.

Aleph. How came this city, once so full of people, to now be abandoned and empty? The mistress of nations is a sorrowful widow: whoever has commanded so many tribes is subject to tribute.

In reading the translation from Latin of François Couperin's *First Tenebrae Lesson*, Tiresias, possessed at the time by an unpopular skepticism and considered paranoid about the 9/11 attacks, sipped on her/his confusion.

In those days, Baroque music kept him/her company when s/he returned from her/his evenings on duty in emergency. Sometimes as a woman, sometimes as a man, but never somewhere between the two bodily states, s/he eased the sharp or dull pain of people who had the personal courage to wait their turn. Caught up in a combination of stress and banality, from laughter lost with the nurses to repressed sorrow, from lives saved by trivial nonsense (which is what s/he thought of the standard treatments administered, the well-learned routines) to readjustments of the humerus in its socket (dis-

113

located shoulder) and a pneumothorax, the emergency doctor treated pain without dealing with her/his anxiety. Deference, professionalism, detachment, and efficiency directed his/her actions, comments, advice, and recommendations.

Once home, alone in her/his new condo on Marie-Anne, eyes closed on his/her padded Barcelona chair, s/he breathed in the emotional density of Couperin's music before going to bed. More than just a relaxing moment, it was a kind of atheist meditation, sustained by the austere beauty of the human voice wrapped around words of lament.

In this way, s/he withdrew from what s/he called "the general madness," the agitated, trigger-happy attitude of our neighbours to the south, of course deploring the death of more than three thousand people in the attack, but even more the belligerent, rapacious response to this civilizational tragedy. S/he rarely paid attention to conspiracy theories—delusional psychoses tacked onto people's prejudices—but on the subject of 9/11, s/he was skeptical, furious, stunned, and full of doubt. Naturally, s/he didn't dare share this with her/his colleagues, medical friends, or loved ones, afraid of sounding like a lunatic, so adamantly was the mainstream media in a mode of "legitimate vengeance" or "let's see what the official investigation turns up before deciding," but this is when s/he lost (s/he later admitted) what little faith s/he still had in politics in general.

His/her cynicism was well underway, and the headaches followed suit.

Was saving people from the "general madness" more urgent than *mending the living*[3]?

Tiresias knew s/he didn't have to ask this kind of polarizing question. Nevertheless, in the privacy of her/his home, with its three IKEA bookcases and two tall CD towers, s/he dwelt on it.

The Christopher Hogwood ensemble, on the Oiseau-Lyre label (1991), played Couperin's *First Tenebrae Lesson* on repeat. The voice of Carolyn Emma Kirkby flowed from the sound system in a soft blaze, releasing its particular smoke.

The solidification process of the inner membrane that protects one from the onslaught of chaos took its course. Nanoparticles of confidence in life, a needed serenity, and a healthy rebalance of belief rewove the precious fabric of kindness, the soft and supple tissue that makes good human relationships possible. S/he educated her/his cynicism, made it socially acceptable, by rubbing it against works brandishing *vanitas vanitatum*. Our vanity (dust that will return to dust) evoked by many traditional images: Hans Holbein's small, anamorphic skull, Balthasar van der Ast's rotting fruit (ca. 1593), or Jacopo de' Barbari's iron gloves and dead partridge nailed to a wall by an arrow (ca. 1440).

The *Tenebrae Lessons* are the musical equivalent of

---

3. The title of a superb novel by French author Maylis de Kerangal (translated by Jessica Moore) about twenty-four hours in the life of a transplanted heart.

these small, existential tableaux helping us to meditate on death.

Rid of his/her knife-shaped ideas, Tiresias could then slip into the night.

The bed as a form of hospitality without expectations. Available, like generous love.

Sandrine and Ninelle the young mom, 2001

November 17, 2001. Sandrine Berthiaume-Côté is one month old.

Messy apartment, the baby's room, the mother an escapee or, rather, ecstatically lit up by symbiosis. Child/breastfeeding symbiosis, mother's body/closed eyes symbiosis.

On the night table, de Beauvoir's letters to her lover, Nelson Algren. For Ninelle, the philosopher's lucidity, her clear, frank thinking, her refusal to marry are benevolent ramparts around her baby's future. De Beauvoir writes about the books she is reading, her literary encounters, and of course her love for the handsome Communist novelist in Chicago. Ninelle finishes reading a letter from 1948 in which the "Beaver" criticizes Faulkner for being overly "tragic," fundamentally bleak, offering no way out. Seeing life only under the guise of tragedy glosses over a large part if its natural expressions. The long, tranquil turquoise river spreading its blanket of indifference, the broad shore of possibility accessible to all do not seem to interest the Southern writer. Watching her daughter sleep, hair like grass seed tossed on fertile soil, the musician is moved. An idea enters her mind, an extension of her reading.

Nothing is tragic, everything is contingent.

She decides to write it down, as it seems to adequately sum up what she thinks about life.

While her baby sleeps, she pens her few words in the margin of her copy of *A Transatlantic Love Affair: Letters to Nelson Algren*, next to the passage on Faulkner. The pages of her book are dog-eared, but she also uses it as a paperweight, carrying it with her everywhere she feeds her daughter—in the living room, in the kitchen, in bed. She's also slipped into de Beauvoir's book a sheet of paper listing famous births and deaths as well as major historical events associated with Sandrine's birthdate. Like an amulet.

Sandrine shares a birthdate with Evel Knievel, the Singing Nun, Rita Hayworth, Montgomery Clift, John Paul I, and Eminem. A date for daredevil artists and personalities, Ninelle thinks. An incongruous mix that ultimately doesn't tell us anything about people born on October 17, but provides fertile terrain for astrology. The human interpretation machine looks very much like a bingo cage, tossing fifty possible scenarios and omitting a billion others.

A brand-new site, Wikipedia, caught her attention this fall. A French version of the platform recently became available. This is where she found the information about her daughter's birthdate.

Tiresias, 2012—Social and amorous thunder and lightning

Collège de Valleyfield.

Someone gets up to speak, some short, unknown Tintin. He says:

> First, I think it's important to remember why we're here today, why we're obliged to talk about a strike. We're here because we're faced with one of the worst threats to the accessibility of higher education in the history of Quebec.[4]

The day before, in Barcelona, painter and sculptor Antoni Tàpies died, an artist who used non-noble materials in his work well before Arte Povera: earth, glass, torn fabric, marble dust, organic matter. Tapiès's canvases are torn, scratched, punctured, attesting to the pure state of active suffering, the hostile, animal gesture that comes before a violent death.

"Set Fire to the Rain," "Rolling in the Deep" (and soon, toward August, "Skyfall") are monopolizing commercial radio stations and continuing to feed the phenomenal success of young Adele.

The year 2012 will be one of excesses, and everyone knows it without actually being able to say in what way.

---

4. Gabriel Nadeau-Dubois, *In Defiance*, trans. Lazer Lederhendler (Toronto: Between the Lines, 2013), 13.

In Montreal, the winter is mild. Tiresias is strolling down Saint Denis Street, in no hurry. Everyone is walking on automatic pilot, but she glances up at the sky now and again, a sky that leaves her uninspired. Feeling uninspired by the sky is, in her opinion, a reason to linger and gaze at it for a while longer. She walks with her graphite-coloured coat unzipped, as the Canada Goose parka (Selkirk model) holds in too much heat close to her body.

A fan of Quebec films, and with a few free hours before her, she has decided to go see Kim Nguyen's *War Witch* at the Quartier Latin cinema. The film features a child soldier narrating, to her unborn baby, the tragic story of her life as an orphan after her parents are killed. A preteen by North American standards, but a young woman ready for the roughness of war, the taste of death, and senseless violence in a fictional African country corrupted by cruel and brutal rebel forces. Village taken, parents slaughtered, kids abducted, dreams burned and buried in lime.

Tiresias's idea in seeing the film is to put her usefulness, her vocation, into perspective. She helps many children keep their minds in childhood for as long as possible, by constantly fertilizing the barren fields of their bodies promised to the realm of ghosts. She battles the inevitable by reshuffling the cards of their destinies, playing the apprentice sorcerer, while aiming her scientific Kalashnikov at the debilitating symptoms and discomfort of a deadly disease. Childhood is not a given for everyone. Childhood is a luxury of rich countries. She knows this. He knows this. But fighting for the privilege of playing for a while longer, putting off debilitating responsibilities, commonplace economic slavery, the pomp of a successful social life according to constantly changing criteria, is for him a rebellious act, a political stance that makes the world's final climax stand in for philosophy.

In the theatre, a handful of cinephiles. In contrast to films made to entertain and undermined by a fascination for derisive destinies, Quebec cinema preaches its distinct realism. On par with life, on par with people's misfortune, this socially engaged cinema exhausts fans of *X-Men*, *Green Lantern*, or Tom Cruise.

Scanning the room for want of something to do, Tiresias's eyes come to rest on a slender thirty-year-old with an oval face and narrow shoulders. The colour of oolong, the man's skin takes on a bluish tint when the light of the screen reflects on it. A profound peace emanates from him.

Sensuality begins with smells and micro-expressions.

After the film, all the elements that make a person intriguing amass to form a global impression in Tiresias's senses as he exits the theatre.

What should I do to draw this man's attention?

Inspired by je-ne-sais-quoi, Tiresias takes his iPhone 5s out of his pocket and drops it. The man makes a pirouette and lateral movement, then stops. Looking for the source of the disruption, he takes a second to turn around and notices Tiresias, who indicates surprise and irritation in the same breath. The man's long pianist hand touches the floor briefly before grabbing the brand-name object and asking Tiresias: "Do you often get angry at Steve Jobs?"

The surprising question, his amused tone and sense of humour, seduce Tiresias.

The unusual encounter is so stimulating for them

both that they exchange names and friend each other on Facebook the very next day.

Tiresias has just met Hermenegild Mukanyonga.

*

The same evening, at Collège de Valleyfield, the students vote in favour of the strike: 460 to 448.

> A deafening clamour broke out. Instinctively, Maxime and I turned to face each other. "We're on strike!" he shouted with his hands in the air and tears welling up in his eyes. I clambered over the row of seats that stood between us and jumped into his arms. "We're on strike! We're on strike!" he repeated. Twelve votes. We had won by a margin of twelve votes."[5]

---

5. Ibid., 15.

Night at the Emily Dickinson Home, 2012

The computer screen casts a soft glow. Twelve images of sleeping children are a reminder that twelve sick children live here. At the nurses' station in the Emily Dickinson Home, nighttime is a strange film.

The daytime, while not exactly stormy, is a ballet of living beings in liquid silence, now and then clouded by bubbles of noise, groans, compulsive enthusiasm, and muffled vitality. Down's syndrome and leukemic children, those suffering from Lowe syndrome, Lou Gehrig's disease, Hutchinson-Gilford progeria syndrome, genetic malformations, and two or three other rare diseases—the names of which won't tell you anything—walk up and down the centre's corridors, go out to Jean Duceppe Park, discover the very partial or minimal animation that can still be called "being alive." Some of them, less hindered by hypotonia or hypertonia, the degeneration of their bones, their liver, their heart, or their senses, run in the corridor-gymnasium, using their apparatus of sensorial awareness, throwing the volunteers and orderlies off balance.

But at night, the place seems deserted. Like in a Roy Andersson film. Static shot filmed in studio, with actors confined to specific locations, forbidden from stirring unduly. At night, the fiction's volume is lowered. The theatre of relationships breaks down. Those who have trouble

123

sleeping, afflicted by convulsions or spasms, are placed in a net bed, a tent of white fabric and mesh walls in a half-moon shape that opens by a zipper. A mosquito net with an identification number.

Sandrine is on the screen, lower left-hand side; she sleeps with no surprises or problems. Her dreams take place in the Blue Whale Room, right across from the bathroom lab, the room for cleaning bodies. An astonishing calm reigns, a silence of stone.

A young blond woman with an immaculate uniform and access card is reading a book, periodically glimpsing at the surveillance camera images.

> The first pogroms against the Tutsis broke out on All Saints' Day, 1959. The machinery of the genocide had been set into motion. It would never stop. Until the final solution, it would never stop.[6]

Historical horrors, shocking real-life events, fears, fantastical adventures, and a deconstruction of the ennui of living occupied both the night nurse and the dreamers in the rooms of the Emily Dickinson Home.

The BHM patient lifts at rest, their frames empty, the pool deserted, the toys stored away, all noise abated. Describing silence is a task for a gourmet. The reality taster expresses whatever nuances are needed to accurately depict the silence taking over at night. Every silence has its personality, perfume, rhythm, physiognomy, and tex-

---

6. Scholastique Mukasonga, *Cockroaches*, trans. Jordan Stump (New York: Archipelago Books, 2016), 15.

ture. The silence of a wintry plain, far from urban areas. The silence of "once upon a time," before we tell a fairy tale without words. The silence that leads to nothing other than the return of the day. The silence of completeness.

The staff and nurses are not fools, however. Anything can happen at night: intense pain, the rapid deterioration of a child's vital functions, and neurological laughter, a reflex caused by electricity in the brain of certain residents sunken into a strange sleep. A mechanical, artificial laughter that erupts at three in the morning, escaping unawares from a young resident's mouth. The hiccups and deluge of mockery aimed at the world, at the substance of nothingness, which always takes the night staff by surprise when they're on call for the first time. Neurological laughter is a kind of werewolf that creates legends, rarely encountered but fuelling talk among the staff. A paper-plate werewolf painted in gouache that makes the heart beat faster when it first appears and continues to perturb in subsequent visits.

On this night of May 2012, there's no anomaly. Other than that of the world, which doesn't care whether we name it or not.

Tiresias, 2012—Human hatred, cruelty, and sensuality

Hatred and cruelty do not have a natural ecosystem.

They are unstable emotions that move around a great deal. They surface around the globe, here and there, at the whim of people's psychoses, in moments of panic or in response to barbaric acts. Nature's economy simply could not function 100 per cent on this destructive diet. The human being was designed to be idle. Those who are denied idleness gradually become aggressive, then vengeful and, ultimately, cruel. The process of acclimatizing to the frustrations that life throws our way ends, in most cases, in scandalmongering, meanness, gossip, and base hypocrisy. Humans being what they are, they must learn to decompress and funnel their mental release. True hatred and cruelty require too much concentration, too much organization, to become an option worth considering.

Hermenegild Mukanyonga was trying to explain to Tiresias what the ripe fruit of racial hatred can look like. He had left Rwanda in 1992, two years before the genocide. From a Western perspective, it was difficult to understand. But if one had to oversimplify it, for the sake of a lively conversation, between two bites of bread and a good glass of wine, Hermenegild Mukanyonga need only have said: "It all started with the West and colonization."

Tiresias, naked in hir host's bed, was listening attentively to his remarks. S/he recalled the involvement of a Swiss archbishop, a certain André Perraudin, who, in order to re-establish a semblance of social justice, had written the following in a "Pastoral Letter" in 1959:

> In our Rwanda, differences and social inequalities are to a large extent related to differences in race, in the sense that the wealth on the one hand and political and even judicial power on the other hand, are to a considerable extent in the hands of people of the same race.

And so it came to pass that a few years later, raised to power by various factors, including Perraudin's influence, Kayibanda's party—the Party for Hutu Emancipation (the Parmehutu)—mutated into a machine for killing the Tutsis.

Very soon, hatred crystalized into a desire to kill, a will to eradicate a whole race, a development of genocidal thinking. Yet to go from politics to murder is a limit that people rarely cross.

Tiresias's lover, educated, slim, and of rare beauty, born in 1977 near Kigali, had sensed the political heat of the 1990s, once the Tutsis, exiled in Burundi after the massacres of the 1960s, had returned. In 1990, a knife between the teeth, seething rage, and hatred represented the most common resources in a country that, for several decades, had seen relative peace and calm reign between the ethnic groups, which were not entirely separate since a Hutu could become a Tutsi and a Tutsi, a Hutu. In the past, the designation of "Tutsi" was reserved for those who owned and took care of cattle, and "Hutu" for those who farmed fields. They all spoke the same two languages, Kinyarwanda and Rundi. Inter-ethnic marriages were common until the arrival of German and then Belgian colonizers. Before this era, the majority of the population, composed of over 85 per cent Hutu, did not represent a threat for the Tutsi minority, who nevertheless wielded most of the levers of power.

In the region around Nyamata, in the early 1960s, the first massacres of the Tutsis took place. Hermenegild had heard about it from his mother, who had fled from it. Government helicopters flew low over the huts, flushing out the *inyenzi*—the so-called "cockroaches" in the propaganda of the racist government in power—by shooting them from above. Truckloads of soldiers swelled the patrols in Nyamata, launching grenades at groups of Tutsi children walking to school, and gathering up fathers and sons who were never seen again. The soldiers took care of this organized ethnic cleansing with diligence and professionalism.

The conversation continued over breakfast, around a few perfectly ripe mangoes and bananas. As Hermenegild was biting into a fruit, Tiresias asked him a question that had been nagging hir.

—But how did this ethnic violence translate into daily life?

Mango juice glazing the corners of his mouth, and sucking up some of the liquid pearling his lips, he answered.

—It was like a Ku Klux Klan atmosphere. Something heavy, constant, muted, weighing on everything all the time, without anyone ever talking frankly about the magnitude of the threat. Racist jokes, spitting, looks that kill, all very commonplace under the circumstances. But as of 1990, everything got worse.

—Worse? You mean everybody went mad!

—Yes, yes! I know that it all sounds surreal! But if a population lives in a surreal, racist climate for over thirty years, and then garbage radio stations, like the infamous and hateful Mille Collines, in the pocket of genocidal authorities, start inciting people to murder and kill, sparks fly, as you like to say here! (*Knowing smile.*)

Hermenegild went on.

—And it's always more complicated than we think. The Hutus don't hold a monopoly over cruelty. The Tutsis massacred Hutu refugee camps in Burundi. The Rwandan Patriotic Front committed war crimes in north Rwanda. The Tutsi government, in power as of 1995, is not clean as snow. We shouldn't be naive, so much hatred demands vengeance. A million Tutsis were massacred by machetes, but hundreds of thousands of Hutus paid with their lives for the Tutsi persecution. Seriously, everyone is guilty of having thought of it, if not of having done it. I'm no better, even if I never took up arms. It's the polluting of our ideas that makes life impossible. My life became impossible, and I had to do something, get out, escape that dump of stinking hate...

Sipping their coffees, Tiresias and Hermenegild continued to talk politics and human madness. Despite the serious nature of their remarks, the conversation remained good-natured, sprinkled with laughter and hands caressing shoulders and necks, faces and hips.

A few sexual nights spent with this man had greatly

satisfied Tiresias. The combination of sensual friend-
ship, engaging conversations, and moments so intimate
that they were not lost in severe solitude had thrilled the
doctor.

Puncto reflexionis, 2015

[OUR COMMON ORIGIN AS AN EPILOGUE INSERTED IN THE BODY OF THE TEXT]

Lokiarchaeota.

This is the name that a team of scientists gave it.

Loki, for friends.

Loki is our first father, first mother, first ancestor, a lot less glam than Darwin and his monkey, living in the deep sea, more than two kilometres below the liquid surface of the Atlantic Ocean. Loki is a prokaryote equipped with all the tools it needs to become an eukaryote. In a way, Loki is the missing link. The alpha that led to our omega, the living drop that enabled the development of animal and vegetal diversity on earth.

Two-point-one billion years ago, before the birth of Mario Lemieux, Marlon Brando, Joyce, Diderot, Shakespeare, Plato, Nebuchadnezzar, Jesus Christ, Maimonides, Gilgamesh, Lucy, the first tiger, the first fish, the axolotl, the nautilus, in the melting pot of life on earth, when the very first fungi, the very first bacteria formed, Loki existed. Loki is a hybrid, a useful transition between a single-celled being and a multi-celled organism. In brief, it is the brother, sister, and ancestor of everyone, of all living, moving elements fed by photosynthesis, crawling, blinking, eyeless, multiplying through rhizomes or mycelia.

We are all Loki's children.

The cat sleeping on the chair, the plant sunbathing on

the veranda, the fruit in one fridge drawer, the vegetables in the other, the eggs in the tray holder specifically designed for this purpose, the bacteria in the throat, the esophagus, the stomach, the eyes, on skin, on teeth, the fruit fly in the kitchen, lost and looking for sugar, the microscopic fungus found everywhere in our environment and bodies, all of us, we are all Loki's children.

We are all Loki's great-great-great-great x 10^{14} grandchildren.

For 2.1 billion years, Loki has been serially reproducing without evolving into something other than the repetition of its genetic fibre. It has specialized. It lives only in the Mid-Atlantic Ridge, close to hydrothermal vents. It hasn't evolved; it has fiercely kept its ecological niche. Who would want to complain about it or criticize it? It's our ancestor, and we owe it a respect far beyond all the known, grandiose rites for honouring our ancestors, all ethnocultural expressions of this kind on earth. Its existence is beyond homage, a first-hand testimony for all international legal projects that want to formulate the rights of nature. The first bacteria or cells, the first multi-celled organisms, benefited from the ingenuity of its composition, from the genetic toolbox that Loki gave them to come into the world.

Loki is the "helping hand of chance" that made our emergence as a species possible. The ecosystem we now call Earth or Gaia or Turtle Island, in order to unite all its descendants, developed thanks to Loki.

*

The article on Loki appeared in an issue of the prestigious science journal *Nature* in May 2015. Almost three years have passed since we lost trace of the flickering, gynandromorphic doctor who went by the name of Tiresias. They too a descendent of Loki. Their condo lies empty. No debit or credit transaction has been recorded since their disappearance. Their 2012 income tax has never been filed. Their friends and acquaintances have not received any phone call, visit, email, or text, any contact by Skype or Messenger. After a three-year investigation, the Montreal police have decided to file the case in binder 17.

A discreet but forthright detective would tell you that, generally speaking, a case file is relegated to binder 17 because there's little chance of it being solved. The same detective would tell you that binder 17 is nothing less than a space-time vortex.

In short, binder 17 means oblivion.

The oblivion to which we give a name.

Sandrine, 2010—Day of the diagnosis

Fatigue. The kind that saps the body, robs it of its vital energy.

Fatigue for no reason, persistent, tortuous, insidious. At the first innocuous signs of irregularity, the arrival of Mister Illness doesn't always entail outlandish symptoms.

In early 2010, overwhelming, crushing fatigue slayed Sandrine. Initially, her friends thought her lazy, checked out. In the courtyard of her new school, located less than a kilometre from her aunt's apartment where she now lived, she received snowballs without reacting. Snow accumulated on her like on an abandoned stump. Soon after, she was no longer considered a viable game partner. They tolerated her sitting down or they forgot about her. Two or three times she went to see the school nurse so she could stretch out on a sofa in her office for a few minutes.

A long time passed before anyone thought of getting tests and bloodwork done. Throughout the process, Evelyne, the spinster aunt, tried to soothe her niece's worry as best she could.

Then, the diagnosis was given.

As heavy as a guilty verdict. The doctor at the Children's Hospital was categorical. Not even awkward about it. He had acquired a curious ease in announcing the worst news using a tone of voice and word choice that delayed the effect of the fatal prognosis. Hypnotized, Evelyne opened her mouth to say something, but to no avail. No sound came from her lips. Her stomach rebelled for a few seconds.

Shocked by the pronouncement of her death, Sandrine didn't cry right away. She had an innocuous reflex. She said to her aunt: "I hope that at least you'll make me some good cheese nachos tonight!" Sandrine had the rest of the following week and the one after to cry, punch her bed, beat the walls, laugh at it all, then cry again. But the day she found out that she would soon die, she asked Evelyne for her famous cheese nachos.

Tiresias, 2003—Montreal's first pediatric palliative care conference

Three hundred people have gathered at Montreal's first pediatric palliative care conference. Tiresias is reading a book of poetry by Dominique Robert while waiting for the next presenter.

> I'm alone
> in a store
> that sells everything:
> sky, trees, clouds, wind, night, animals
>
> I know that birds fly
> just long enough
> to keep reality
> from focusing on them
>
> I'm dying of slowness
> because my presence must stay
> exactly where it is[7]

Pared down and meditative, Robert's poetry reflects the ambiguous nature of realism, of reality, in Tiresias's opinion, despite the sparing use of the words *soul*, *angel*, and *eternity*, which get on her nerves. Tiresias has always read

---

7. Dominique Robert, *Sourires* (Montreal: Les Herbes Rouges, 1997), 14.

and been interested in poetry with a scientific, materialist realism. The phrase that comes to mind is *scientific realism*, that which has no meaning in itself, but which one has to understand, like nature and everything around us, including consciousness, explained according to the latest scientific theories. The beauty of Robert's poetry rests in intuitive but fair descriptions, evoking conscious phenomena, approaching reality as something that is encoded and at the same time designed to be perceived only through the prism of our solitude. Childlike observations stand alongside more intangible impressions.

> Reality
> as the husk around
> man's breath[8]

She underlines this stanza on page forty-two, frowning slightly that the word *man*, all-encompassing, too all-encompassing, is used here. But she knows this is just a detail and the poet is also talking about the male sex and carnal pleasure. Nevertheless, this poem expresses something true about how the brain works, something greatly astounding.

Reality is thin, forming only a fine film before our eyes.

Effects of depth, of past tense, of otherness, of the acoustic environment, of 360-degree vision are produced by our brains before we conceive them. Reality in a nutshell, more or less, a walnut in two parts, cerebral hemispheres separated by a border, shaped like a cauliflower,

8. Ibid, 42.

like coral, like minuscule deltas with potassium and endorphin deposits. An agnostic believing that humans can't somehow access the real substance of the universe, the more Tiresias read, the more she sided with the fiercely atheist camp, the atheists who no longer conceded to the transcendently enlightened. Moral philosophy is simply the exercise of an insidious, perverse power and fear, the last warden acting as the ultimate restriction.

This long reflection led her to reconsider her practice as an emergency doctor and reassess the priorities in her life. Emergency doctors are good garage mechanics for the living: they check the engines, plug away section by section, fix flat tires, do basic auto body repairs, change the mufflers, reassure people about the strange noises made by the bodywork, join universal joints, give advice about the significant corrosion affecting the entire vehicle, ease people's concerns about the car model they can afford. The comparison is certainly flawed, but she isn't looking to glorify her role or place emergency medicine for polytrauma patients on a pedestal.

*

More recently, Tiresias has become interested in pediatric palliative care.

The science is new. Pediatric palliative care has a short history that more or less began in the 1990s. She had waffled between pediatrics and emergency for a long time, choosing the most useful one in the hierarchy of care offered people. Yet she doesn't understand why the frenzy of the living irritates her more and more, why the fury of living, the fury of conquering, this racing pit stop we've all become, is sapping her last resources. She hasn't exactly fallen into a depression; it would be misleading to use such a strong word to describe what is more like an asthenia, a loss of faith in the devotion she's had for human wrecks. Her humanism, however, has not lost any of its vigour, except that she finds herself increasingly wanting to dedicate it to other sorts of people, to children caught in the snares of time, still stuck in the deep-sea floor before the brutal barge of illness rips them away to their due tranquility. Drummer crabs, light crabs, crabs in clusters, genetically worn-down since birth, crooked legs, brain going backwards, net squeezing their bodies like a hand squeezing a dried orange.

She doesn't yet know that in 2008, upon the opening of the Emily Dickinson Home, she will reorient her career and shift gears. A decision unwittingly taken years ago that requires her to follow an unconscious route so she can gradually adjust the coherence of her new life narrative.

Life resembles a fairy tale in the making.

We all need to find our big bad wolf, our Little Thumb, our Hansel and our Gretel, our confused grasshopper, or our sensitive dragon. The subconscious tries to write a story that holds together and copies from existing models. We have to invent a story, propose some just punishment, some reasonable trauma, a well-known event that will force the train to change tracks. A decision always needs a reason. Our body takes most of its decisions without consulting us, and our consciousness then makes up stories to get accustomed to them.

For Tiresias, it will be a poignant heartbreak that, in 2008, will convince her to act.

Revolutions, revolts, changes of course exist as potential, for years seeping into our bodies steeped in habits, in the always present future, without us scratching the surface, afraid of tempting fate, making our lottery ticket null and void.

> Solitude is a temple
> where resplendent
> wounds watch me
> with the eyes of a child
> acquainted with symbols[9]

---

9. Ibid.

Sandrine, 2012—Wheelchair

With a hand on the hydraulic jack, the porter monitors the slow rise of the painted metal platform. The yard of the Emily Dickinson Home features a few swings, including a huge red wheelchair swing that's shaped like a canopy and can hold a wheelchair and its occupant.

The porter, always smiling, often stroking Sandrine's arm, begins to rock her. Small, gentle pushes, enough to move the apparatus of assorted alloys, pistons, rubber wheels, sealant; the painful package of thin, brittle bones cast into comfortable polymer layers, placed in an ingenious suspension system, all connected to a head that speaks less and less. A head that hurts, rests, thinks a little, is sometimes delirious, and for which all effort is made, by all means available in modern pharmacopoeia, to avoid a level of unbearable suffering.

Lately, Sandrine no longer walks. She mumbles words, watches movies, not all the way to the end, still loves music, hears what others say to her, and drinks in the voices of all who interact with her. Extensive logistical support is required to offer her recreational activities worthy of the name, sunny days consistent with the warmth of the adjective, full days with their share of affection and amusing surprises.

The huge swing has not been designed to trace an extravagant arc. The heavy apparatus rocks with a safe slowness, like the pendulum of a grandfather clock in a Bavarian house. A strange pendulum that, instead of evacuating existence, makes existence part of its paradoxical countdown. Most physicists acknowledge that the passing of time is an illusion, and so much the better that this illusion gives us a vivid impression of having the last word on how our days unfold. Besides, days unfold because they too are attached to a space-time structure, a considerable, supposedly finite page on which we appear like high-voltage puppets. Noisy drones, flashes of light, vectors of consciousness, artists of the absurd, and finicky, luminescent assemblages on stone bases. That's all we are.

Every life is a parallel universe accessible only through a story, a series of snapshots, gossip, scribbles, or moving images.

Sandrine will never know it, but someone is in the process of writing what she was, what she represents, how her life tube, her tunnel of earthly purpose, her bubble of Otherness, her helmet of decibels and perceptions, have affected the few members of her species fortunate enough to know her. How her life, like that of every person, has been complete. Despite the charade of glorious destinies that make one despise oneself, despite the lightness of destinies less brutal than one's own, fully aware of the completeness of one's life, more condensed, more compressed than others' but in which decisive experiences, essential emotions, will have existed in other ways. Steep Slope is surely the name of her life. But thanks to the power of concentration and imagination, everything in this arid realm can become green for a time.

Imagination is the second doctor on call twenty-four hours a day at the Emily Dickinson Home.

The sardine-can story of young Berthiaume-Côté's life is essentially an ode to the beauty that keeps flowing through the mesh of the net: small joys, fine smiles, a feeling of presence when the only things left that matter are active listening and a willingness to enjoy any pleasures still available to us.

Cioran would have spit on so much humanitarian perseverance, but Cioran never lived, he only thought. And here, at the Emily Dickinson Home, they do nothing but live.

Young Tiresias, 1976

The United States Bicentennial, Washington.

In front of a life-size mammoth at the Smithsonian National Museum of Natural History, young Tiresias is mulling things over. A child, barely seven years old, and he's full of questions. These extravagant creatures with majestic skeletons never existed in his lifetime. The past is something we fossilize, transform into treasure or curse, put on display.

His eyes riveted on the enormous joints of the pachyderm's leg reanimate the beast, infuse life into its bone structures. How did the legs work? Why do they look like those of other species that exist today? Why is the mammoth so similar to the elephant? Questions that will soon find some answers on the museum labels and in the book his father will buy him at the gift shop.

Propelled by the father's interest in history, the whole family has driven south in a metallic-olive station wagon with faux-wood panelling to reach the birthplace of the United States—Washington, DC, between Maryland and Virginia. A kind of drilling into history, a joyous spill. Tiresias and his sister squabbled on the car's rough, irritatingly green carpet. A playing field and reading sandbox where they rolled Yahtzee dice, played cards, but also flipped through colouring books, crossword and puzzle magazines. Songs on the radio, each more sleep inducing than the next. Barry Manilow's uninspiring "I Write the Songs," haggardly slow and bombastically mannered. Words trying to personify music. Nothing to grab the attention of the parents, who prefer French pop, or the children, who are more interested in the Beatles.

> I've been alive forever
> And I wrote the very first song
> I put the words and the melodies together
> I am music
> And I write the songs

As soon as Tiresias's father tuned in to the words on an American station (people said "American" even back then), he groaned a bit and turned off the radio. The small family group then had to endure the silence for kilometres. Until a rest area, hot-dog stand, or deli provided new stimulation to the inhabitants of the moving shell.

Manilow's song talks about eternity, the first song ever written, music expressing itself, a rosy prosopopoeia, and at the same time evokes the man's career. A naive evocation dolled up in sequins that earned the sexy crooner thousands of dollars.

Memory is also a goldmine, where we play the same old tunes to sold-out rooms, where we tell stories like nesting dolls that fascinate everyone, the timeline supported by the largest number of listeners. The big narratives that make up our foundations, that observe us from their impressive height, have always been tasked with lumping us together, creating a group effect, that of the pack, the clan, the giant league we call "nation," "race," "country," "language," "gender," "my identity." They have forged ideas that have shaped the face of the earth, destroyed ecosystems, erected massive constructions, launched wars, ostracized some, tortured others. True, they have also produced vast cultural networks, music, literature, medicine, schools, arts in general, and all types of altruistic thought. Nothing is black and white.

As a child, Tiresias swallowed many outlandish or esoteric explanations whenever he needed to find a cause for an unexplained phenomenon, hence his passion for UFOs, legends, and conspiracies. What mattered was finding the big narrative behind the strange phenomenon or one too complex to correspond to a chapter of the overall novel. A childhood keen for answers, attached to possibilities with a brooch. A childhood that hasn't yet had time to react patiently to reality's abyssal depths. For now, young Tiresias, a small, curious boy, has only three main interests: dinosaurs (including mammoths), military history, and unidentified flying objects.

On July 4, 1976, as President Ford is reciting his speech celebrating his country's bicentennial in Philadelphia, Tiresias is at the site of the Battle of Gettysburg, wondering about the role of surgeons in the American Civil War. Spends several minutes glued to a display of instruments in a military medical bag: amputation saw, scalpel, cannulas, rubber tubes, retractors, and tourniquets, as well as other sharp tools of mysterious uses. He daydreams about something not quite defined, achieving some glorious act, saving a life from gangrene, patching a soldier back together. While eating lunch with his family at the famous battle site, he can't stop thinking about it. Gets hung up on a simple question about organ transplant. Why is it possible to transplant a woman's heart to a man's body, but not a woman's hand to a man's body? Why are some organs gendered and others not? Morphologically speaking, are men and women all that different? Just as with African-Americans in the US, why have these supposed differences been used as a pretext for segregation, an alibi for oppression, which he considers incredibly ridiculous and inappropriate?

While chewing on these intimate questions, which he can't share with his sister, too much of a teaser, or his parents, too pragmatic, he starts to measure the bitterness that comes when one begins to get increasingly farther from the big, common narrative. The great, richly adorned smokescreen that gives people a will to live and goals to reach, and colours every moment of their existence, is similar to superhero cartoons that encourage them to excel in a world peopled by good citizens and punished evildoers.

At the same time in Philadelphia, President Ford, Nixon's successor after the Watergate scandal, is halfway through his speech.

During his short political career, Gerald R. Ford appointed George H. W. Bush (the father) as the American ambassador to China, then as head of the CIA in 1975; he sought out Donald Rumsfeld and made him Secretary of Defense and had the flair to choose a young Wyoming politician, Dick Cheney, as Chief of Staff. On September 5, 1975, he survived an assassination attempt. Lynette "Squeaky" Fromme, a follower of Charles

Manson, pointed a gun at Ford but was disarmed by a Secret Service agent.

While young Tiresias is eating his ham sandwich with a double helping of fluorescent mustard and a leaf of iceberg lettuce, Gerald R. Ford is pronouncing the following words, commemorating the United States Bicentennial of independence:

> It is good to know that in our own lifetime we have taken part in the growth of freedom and in the expansion of equality which began here so long ago. This union of corrected wrongs and expanded rights has brought the blessings of liberty to the 215 million Americans, but the struggle for life, liberty, and the pursuit of happiness is never truly won.[10]

10. http://www.fordlibrarymuseum.gov/library/speeches/760645.asp

Sandrine, 2012—The humanist protocol of the final moments

Sandrine's identity bursts in word bubbles barely stitched together and incoherent gestures. Her body's colony momentarily retakes control.

The medical team acts according to established protocol, tackling three main aspects: pain, obstructing secretions (the death rattle of life's end), and anxiety.

Tiresias is morphologically fluid: a breast pushing against their sweater, a testicle appearing in their sexual flickering, pelvis and hip growing and contracting, extra weight arising and subsiding, penis coming and going between legs and labia, all the sexual markers waltzing with evident anarchy inside their entrails being pulled in all directions without anyone on the medical team taking any notice. A bit like Samantha in *Bewitched* (the sympathetic sorceress in the 1960s American sitcom, a small suburban firefly corresponding to the dusty fantasy of a playful and successful patriarchal marriage), all the bodily magic tricks are perceived by only one other person apart from the real party of interest. In the case of the TV series, only her husband knows her secret.

Sandrine alone is aware of Tiresias's sexual flickering. A young child who, at this stage of life, since we're still speaking of her life, doesn't care about the appearance of the doctor treating her.

Eleven-thirty p.m. Aunt Evelyne is at her bedside, gently palpating her arm without touching the depths of pain eased by opiates. She makes slow circles, focusing on the young skin ready to slip into death at any moment.

The death rattle is increasing in frequency, and Tiresias authorizes the nurses to give Sandrine a dose of Robinul, which will partly reduce the salivary secretions creating it. To die without excessive suffering, to control the symphony of agonizing symptoms, discomfort, and fear related to life's end is no small task.

Tiresias is constantly suppressing preposterous ideas in an effort to remain professional, never sharing with their close ones or team the desire they sometimes have to resuscitate children, to stop death in its tracks like a ridiculous knight/valiant amazon in a tale of ageless prince/great female explorer. For a few seconds, they see themself leave gravitational space-time, generally considered the only reality, and sit on a lonely chair in a cinematographic desert. There, in direct contact with the vital ebb and flow determining who will survive and who will die, they witness a surrealist spectacle. Thousands of luminous waves and rays, enlivened with colour, interspersed with strings of fading light, gradually go out. Tiresias grabs a hesitant, almost grey thread and miraculously joins it with another bright yellow, radiant wave. In their daydreaming hands, these two lifelines (childish abstractions of our fate) fuse. Skeins of atonal music on an arrow sash, a Bayeux Tapestry, quantum hair floating in the electric wind of atoms. It is but one point in space-time and in all that flows in this microcosm. Tiresias has just enough time to retain an emotion they feel despite themself before being swept along by the ultrafast domino fall of their neural circuits. The full execution of routine sadness arrests on their features.

Two seconds of escape, two long seconds that remain intimate, secret, precious, and slightly uncomfortable for a great professional of their calibre. This time, a flash of lightning strikes their face. For a thirty-hundredth of a second, while everyone is looking elsewhere, a micro-expression emerges between their eyes, mouth, and nose. A kind of sudden, infinitesimal pause on a steep slope before they plunge into the gelatinous, frigid waters of Lake Melancholia.

Tiresias, 2012—*Puncto reflexionis*

Tiresias sets down a popular science book on the bedside table. This one talks about time. Days end just like mornings. A banal observation, just like night has come. But the idea of a purpose: get to the end of the day.

Pierre de Coubertin gave us a purpose, that of participating in a social, Darwinian adventure modelled on his passion for sports. It was in 1908, at the London Olympic Games, that he felt called upon to define the Olympic ideal, the new economic *doxa*: *The most important thing is not winning but taking part.*

In a way, we are all major players in the Self Olympics, the ordinary Olympics of maximum profit, maximum productivity, and also the maximum of ourselves. On our tiny, personal scale, this madness is barely noticeable, except in the vocabulary we use: "a fresh start," "a breakfast of champions," "a head start," "a price war," "a hero's welcome," to "hit a wall," "show up late," "get off on the right foot," "ruin your health." Hundreds of these expressions form the basis of our own Olympic ideal of contributing to society, being useful to progress, completing our lap around the track by adequately passing the baton to the person coming after us. With the exception of a few oddballs and a handful of anarchists, no one questions the strange idea that we all work to elect the leaders and that ultimately, all our effort, all our inspiration, the purpose of our existence is put toward celebrating and rewarding the leaders, the crème de la crème, without hoping for anything other than "taking part" in this extraordinary pyramid scheme. Taking part in the Social Olympics means helping to elect a separate class of individuals, picking them out from the masses and placing them in the limelight of time eternal, longevity, and felicity. A kind of atheist sacrifice of our thirst for the sun, the game lost from the start to economic forces but in which we have proudly taken part.

The strange logic of business is that it takes an enormous number of losers to support a few winners.

Tiresias, 2012—After Sandrine's death

August 13, 2012, 2:34 p.m.

At this hour, Tiresias is prescribing antibiotics to Sammy, another child in their care struggling with acute sinusitis, a miserable infection he develops twice a year. Terminal illness doesn't drive away the lowly nuisance of common ailments. In contaminated soil, weeds continue to grow. And the work of a doctor in pediatric palliative care is that of a horticulturist and landscaper of the final moments. The palliative care doctor ensures that all residents (the team prefers the term *resident* over *patient*) at the Emily Dickinson Home are able to optimally enjoy their lucid, conscious moments, their moments of being present with themselves and with others, as permitted by the symptoms of their primary illness.

Tiresias, 2012—*Puncto reflexionis*

[TIME IS A STRANGE CONCEPT]

Another night.

Tiresias picks up the popular science book on time, reads two chapters, then sets it down on the bedside table.

Are they a Heraclitean or a Parmenidean?

Do they see time as something that is disjointed, fragmentary, made up of points, like Heraclitus, who saw change as the principal natural law? Or do they understand time like Parmenides, a presocratic for whom change was the illusion, for whom time was unified, subject to being, to an unchanging identity?

Tiresias likes to think we are only a collection of points of presence on a space-time plane. Their scientific inclination makes them lean toward Heraclitus, but their philosophical, poetical inclination finds that Parmenides answers some of their most private questions. For whether we simply take part in the Social Olympics or are the medalists, when can we actually say that life is complete?

What does it mean to have a complete life?

Shim notices the night gently closing in, taking them by the hand toward unknown philosophical realms. In the Social Olympics, Shim is a gold medalist. With a medical degree, Shim will never again need to think about money.

Yet Shim sees the limitations, baseness, and gross injustices of this social Darwinism. How can one find the means to distribute more medals? Furious every time they hear the same old idiotic tune giving some people the right to be called "someone." Shim unabashedly castigates these tactless talkers. Those who drive in their social alienation by hammering the nails of their frustration. "Becoming someone" is everyone's lot, from the residents of the Emily Dickinson Home to Pope Benedict XVI.

In essence, therefore, Tiresias is a Parmenidean. They refuse anyone the advantages of privileged scenarios; they encourage a general human identity, edifying in itself, dignified, unencumbered by the slag of change, unwavering.

There are no winners or participants, only beings mounted on trestles with their billions of cells, crossing space-time, feeling the present according to their own parallel universe, and leaving the time plane when the resources for regenerating their consciousness dry up and die.

Shim's humanism as a doctor focused on others has convinced them that their life, the life of Madonna, Alexander Fleming, Julie Payette, Cicero, Patrice Lumumba, Louis Pasteur, or René Lévesque harbours the same degree of completeness as that of Sandrine, Sammy, or Ahmed.

Arriving at this profound intuition, which they don't quite know how to clearly articulate since it's part of a nucleus of embryonic ideas that stimulate them, Tiresias turns off the green lamp and comfortably sinks into the indeterminacy of dreams.

Ninelle, 2012—The last gift

Ninelle takes the box being handed to her.

The only mode of communication that now connects her to the external world is her Artaudian logorrhoea. The pages of her notebooks address the great Other in oneself, the one who, if we have digested the social spotlight, invents others, creates a reassuring binary world, making us into characters among other complex, autonomous ones.

The charge nurse, responsible for the mail, delivers the package to her in a slow, respectful manner. Simone Lecuvillier knows, suspects, imagines that a box like this, of such considerable weight, containing a small, heavy present from the Emily Dickinson Home, is not some secret trifle. Used to extrapolating patients' wishes, piecing together a scenario from confusing words, guessing the presence of pain from repetitive gestures, her intuition has examined the package addressed to the pianist on the floor. She is definitely not going to leave her patient alone with this box. Something gravely serious is going on. She's no fool. Opening this Pandora's box will cause a scene, a drop in blood pressure, and something else she hasn't yet imagined but that her laser-sharp insight—concerned about the many sudden aspects of reality inflicted on fragile minds—can foresee.

Ninelle unhurriedly tears up the Kraft wrapping paper,

unveiling the box in question. A golden box with a pink ribbon. The cover is not sealed. Due to some resistance caused by the air suction between the panels of the box, Ninelle has to momentarily strain before making the contents appear.

On a small nest of paper trimmings, placed on a foam cushion, rests a plaster cast. A tile of dry white plaster, approximately twenty by twenty centimetres long. At the centre of this strange handicraft, a handprint.

Simone Lecuvillier holds back tears, understanding what's happening. She clears her throat. Her emotion thus expressed.

Ninelle doesn't move. Takes the *memory object*, as it is duly described in the brief letter included with the package. She rubs the five-finger negative against her cheek, a vague copy of our ancestors' first works in the caves around the Mediterranean more than one hundred thousand years ago. The mother plays for a few moments with the mould of her daughter's hand. Puts it on the bed. Stretches her legs and gets up. Grabs her Hilroy Québec notebook from the desk.

The nurse waits, still on alert. Her mind is racing; the whole room seems suspect, altered. Then her eyes calm down, disconnect from some infinitesimal tension, one after another the micro-muscles relax, capillaries relieving the muscle tissue, arresting the automatic influx of blood.

Ninelle is writing. Her Zebra gel ink pen, given to her with the pile of Hilroy Québec notebooks, is activated by her Broca's area, her left hemisphere, and the tendons of her right hand. She writes without rushing, with surprising serenity. When she sets her pen down, having written a few paragraphs, she gets up and takes the route of her main form of consolation, the corridor to the right, then to the left, the stairs leading to the ground floor and the public piano. No one besides herself and a man with unkempt hair sits down on its bench.

As soon as she hears the piano notes spill into the morning air, Simone feels free to look at the notebook.

Today. Today.

I am running with my understanding over the slats of forever, in thin shades of grey, hair bound in tight coils. Patagonia is where people end up, stuffed with honey of sheep or lambs, of animals they raise there on the northern slopes, by the raging sea, the overpowering ocean.

I am dead. Everywhere life parts forests of ferns, emits signals for those willing to hear them. Today, we'll put up dunes before dormant challenges. We'll break sugar with glass.

With my happiness patrol, we'll go live far away where death dwells wisely in holes, at altitudes, before it forces our third eye. Mirror of today. Ambient music of incubation. It's time to feed the animals. It's time to feed today. Come, a bit of cold water and some feed for the polar bear, the white thing with the sick growls, the story of several broods of shrubs over certainty's immaculate reservoir.

Now fades away before today. Now fragments before the animal with the black mouth. Mouth. Fur. Triplets of the continuum.

Out of the surrealist jumble of these lines dumped on the page, the psychiatric nurse retains a few words: *It's time to feed today.*

For her, these words get at the root of the composition's meaning. Overall, it has satisfied her. The tone bears few threats, violent images, or parts of invented weapons attacking the body. She can't decode the patients' extraordinary idioms; this is a skill she doesn't possess. Nevertheless, the bit of text personifying *today* into an animal that one must feed pleases her. On her way to photocopy the page and leave it on the psychiatrist's desk, she hears the notes of Fauré's *Sicilienne* being played with loud elation, with joyous and simultaneously introspective energy, releasing the morning's perfume. Never has Ninelle interpreted the work's melancholic smile in G minor so well. The scene where Mélisande loses her ring in the well, her love in limbo. Fallen fruit.

Puncto reflexionis
[WHAT IS CONSCIOUSNESS?]

No one really knows how consciousness disappears.

In fact, it was only very recently that we established a protocol for identifying death. We staked everything on consciousness. We wagered everything on a glass marble moving inside a huge clay globe. Brain death is now what determines the true hour of decease. When brain activity stops, consciousness no longer exists. According to Francis Crick's Nobel Prize in Physiology, consciousness resides in the claustrum, a thin layer of neural tissue, a poorly known cerebral area. This means that the neural operations responsible for our consciousness have been located.

But no one really knows when we die.

At what time do we die?

No conscientious doctor can answer this question. Tiresias never gets into the matter too seriously; they go into some digression about time, vague and general enough. Between immediately and in three days, between two and a half hours and thirty hours, between one night and two days, between right now and over forty-eight hours, death plays hide-and-seek with the data, the absolute trickster measuring our incomprehensibility of its process, its agony, scoffing at the power of medicine.

The agony of death is not a recognized medical concept. There is little common ground among the various specialists about the end of life.

Not to mention that medical circles are not unanimous on pediatric palliative care. Who can really say whether the gradual process of opiate injections doesn't actually cause a child's death? What aspects of the professional assistance provided up to a child's very last moments support life and what aspects harm it? Do you believe in God? Do you adhere to an organized religion? Which one? Does your religion allow blood transfusions? Is an unassisted natural death and the casual allowance of suffering a necessary passage for the purification of your infant's soul? Isn't life just suffering and ennui? Must we drink from the chalice of painful hardships to the very last drop?

True, at the Emily Dickinson Home, a hospice that welcomes its proteges for a maximum of only thirty days, the choice is clear: ease suffering, alleviate anxiety, provide a sufficient and even excess amount of tenderness and love, offer multi-sensory stimulation that encourages interactions with the environment of the child, families, and care providers by all available means; in short, the care provided at this institution contravenes the principles of dolorism of all religions based on sin, all religions based on an exhausting debt.

Here, no one is born in debt, in a blood pact with the unnameable that must be respected, no one is born with a wish to redress a millennial affront caused when thrown out of the earthly paradise. Here, all children have a right to a complete life, without the lead weight of a draining, merciful activity.

Life has always been more complex than desired by the rules established by the powers that be. Life will always remain a strange ride on the back of our consciousness, stimulated by odours, images, flavours, landscapes, words, sounds, knowledge, the procession of days, and the constant fluctuations in the environment around us. A seasoned eye will see the humanism at work in this hospice where death is named and the body rigorously celebrated with all its genetic deformities and structural malfunctions. Because those who work here feel called upon to offer such service precisely so as to prolong the body's joys, whichever ones still remain, whichever ones are still available, whichever ones validate the child's personality, for as long as possible.

In the realm of ethical doubt, theological prevarications, moral guarantees, and vigorous celestial resentment, one needs to trust in the body—a small vehicle—in the only discernable freedom in this world of titans, this bizarro universe we don't yet understand despite all the subtleties of our conscious apparatus.

Sandrine, July 28, 2012, 3:34 a.m.

At 3:34 a.m., the nurse called Tiresias.

Two hours prior, the medical team had left Sandrine, in stable condition, to fall asleep.

The members of the team could then be at liberty to recharge their batteries, while remaining ready to quickly jump into action in case a respiratory problem, convulsions, or contortions of pain reactivate the emergency treatment protocol.

But at 3:34 a.m., on the nursing station monitor, the simple rattle she released, longer than usual, was her last one.

In the span of ten seconds, her condition went from stable to dead.

No one had expected it to come so soon.

Tiresias, always fooled by the end, pronounced time of death and filled out the legal form designed for this purpose.

The charge nurse wiped away something that had fallen from the inner corner of her left eye, an idea perhaps, a liquid memory, a small refusal to forget.

This is when Tiresias lost their footing, collapsed against the wall, back sliding down to the floor, knees bent, head slumped over.

Who could have anticipated this decline?

No one understands their inner landscape all that well.

Crack, fissure, earthquake, eruption. Having duly completed their duty as doctor, Shim sought refuge in their office, bound to the capriciousness of time.

On July 28, 2012, at 3:34 a.m., a strange metabolic process began to take place in their body.

Sandrine's body, 2012

Rigor mortis.

Rigour is often associated with the concept of debt. A symbolic debt owed to some god, an omnipotent human creditor. The debt then morphs into a demand for moral or economic purity. In the body's case, post-mortem "rigour" concerns only certain principles related to muscles. Roughly speaking, the body stiffens after death. Due to a major malfunctioning of the cells.

Between six and twelve hours after death, the effect is at its peak.

The actin in young Berthiaume-Côté's body resembles that of our eukaryote ancestors; it has practically not evolved. Only an infinitesimal difference exists between the protein that makes us move, activates our muscles, and that of the most ancient types of yeast on earth.

We are so belittled, so confined, so held back by the vivisection of our distinctiveness that all too often we eliminate the beauty we have in common. What unites us to nature in general. What makes us elements of nature. We are Gaia. Continuity is in us, insistent, persistent, without victory or defeat, always active in the illusion of time, in imagined fervour, redistributing our dust over the earth.

Rigor mortis begins in the neck and jaw in the first hours after death, when the extremities are not yet rigid, stiffened into impossible, inextricable positions. This is when the first funeral rite must begin.

As soon as the death certificate was issued, the nurse assigned to this task dipped the dead child's right hand into a small container of fresh plaster. The memory object, the handprint, is the last testimony extracted from a child's body.

This morning, the curtains are open in the Neptune Room.

The preparations are well underway.

From a bony, liquid, spongy structure, Sandrine's body has transformed into a solid oasis, a type of empty stone, a geode.

Soon, the morgue attendants will arrive.

Walking, a vital obsession, 2012

Walking is the best remedy for death.

Faced with a culture of condemnation, accumulating kilometres of space-time brings relief. All Tiresias does now is walk, broiling in July's oven heat, braving the winter squalls, plowing through autumn's cold winds. Since their traumatic breakup with Marthe-Lyster Dessalines, the young computer scientist with the ostentatiously offhand manner, Tiresias has been checking off their reasons for surviving on the form of the living.

All their friends tell them they should see a psychiatrist. The medical team at the Emily Dickinson Home repeats the same refrain, gently, jokingly, between two bites at lunch, on a Post-it note stuck on their office door.

None of it is rational. It's all a tumultuous farce, nothing but gossip, a sudden feeling of exhaustion that springs up who knows when to make up for who knows what. No one blames Tiresias, everyone is understanding and accommodating, no reproof burdens conversations. They hold back, but think it all the same. That Tiresias take time off, chill out. Céline, one of the gangly morning nurses, tells them the same thing with a wry smile: "You don't chill out enough!"

They never wanted kids, all the Tinders in the world don't interest them, for them romantic relationships are slow immersions into a habitus they don't know what to do with. Their sexual life is sporadic; they don't ask for more. They read, listen to music, even write. They have no reason to panic, they're a gold medalist, all has smiled upon them and all will smile upon them. It's in their blood. Everything is settled in them and redundant, there's no miracle context or solution. Having eliminated all economic irritants, the humiliation of unpaid debts, having obtained coveted postings, tasted the pride of adding some small amount of humanism to the cycle of seasons, of making a difference in the lives of hundreds of people, hundreds of children caught in a snare in the forest of genes, they realize that nothing tangible is left, that the whole exciting adventure in the realm of regained dignity, equally redistributed in the affection-starved eyes of everyone, only looks like a convenient mirage.

Shim sees mirages everywhere, turbulent zones in the middle of nowhere. Tiresias laughs it off. Tiresias doesn't care. But that's how it is. The humanistic drops they give out now seem like mere chimeras, cheap sweets. Substances that titillate the taste buds for a few brief moments.

An anxiety sponge, civilization is just a series of add-ons piled on add-ons, earthquake alarms piled on earthquake alarms. Tiresias is starting to overflow. Their organ of love, still at full capacity in their relic-free auditorium with clean walls, keeps bellowing. But their organ of giant pipes, bursting with life, inventing beauty on arid land, planting humanism in places where a lack of happiness becomes a congenital disease, has suddenly lost its musician. No feet or arms are left to activate the machinery of dignity. Shim examines the room forming their own resonance chamber, a legacy left to gather dust, and contemplates the disaster of isolation. Isolated, yet not feeling sorrowful, Shim, they, e sinks into a chair.

The water calls em.

The water demands eir presence.

A liquid silence hums in eir temples.

Eir body gradually transforms into a fluid of identity, a suitable sexual brew, a pact against certainty, laws, rules of all kinds, and our indifference to certain categories of people. Eir body offers a response to every prejudice. Eir body eludes identity nonsense, the protocols of one's appearance in front of others, wages its own battle against the one-track mind, the all-out economic focus. Eir body deconstructs the adverse action of social identity—source of control, symbol of debt—of hateful exchanges, of natural ostracism.

Shim no longer knows who e is, at what gynandromorphic stage eir frenetic metabolic process culminates. Shim is not static, that's all. Or determined either. In essence, e is a consciousness like all others, complex, bisexual, queer, asexual, feminine, masculine, non-binary, but whose body reflects mental mutations.

The entity Tiresias dismisses the individualistic farce, expresses eir natural filiation with Gaia. Recreates the supreme magma where dignity is consubstantial with the substance of all species. Nonchalantly returns to the Ectasian Period, when sexual reproduction first appeared, 1.4 billion years ago.

A roaming wanderer smashing established economic mills and countless binary rationales with eir flickering identity, the entity Tiresias is moving on. On the 191 bus, e is on eir way to Stoney Point Park in Lachine. Around eir almost ectoplasmic manifestations, autumn grips the branches, bending yet unable to break them.

Birth of Tiresias Chauveau, 1969

On August 18, 1969, the eye of Hurricane Camille swept Cuba, Louisiana, Alabama, and Mississippi, carving a path of destruction through the American Southwest, ravaging lands, farms, shaking nature before gradually transforming into a tropical storm.

Hurricane Camille killed 143 people, destabilized a Shell oil platform—the combined effect of a submarine landslide and the storm surge—struck and damaged more than 13,000 homes, wounded 8,900 people. A soulless giant, a battery of wind missiles without conscience, this meteorological turbulence repeatedly assaulted the transit patterns of bystanders in this corner of the world.

A natural disaster is a computer virus first and foremost, one spread by nature to reprogram life in certain parts of the earth, a manifestation of objective chance impacting parts of the living fabric. A climate boil, the hurricane mars the tranquility of our life cycles, driving a dart of discontinuity into the flesh of our limbs. We are not dead yet, but we already feel the external glacial cold claiming the right to arrest our journey to nowhere.

Every second, throughout the world, one hundred events more important than our own life unfold.

Our eyes are not the world. But the world can't do anything without our eyes.

We are needles in the haystack of the universe. We are

the happy parents of a baby with the perfect birth record. We believe in the cult of whatever normally corresponds to a successful life in every isolated microclimate on earth.

We are in Saint-Lambert—well, not quite. We are in a car, driving to Saint-Lambert, returning from the nursery of Charles-Le Moyne Hospital, in Greenfield Park. Louis Chauveau and Madrassa Chauveau, née Bélanger, are returning home with their new, spring-loaded smile. After the CBC news report, they turn off the radio of their white Beetle, fed up with hearing the words *disaster*, *many casualties*, *Camille*, and *rebuilding*.

Their son has just been born, an abstract beauty in a white toque, an unspun silkworm, a red-cheeked thing of cries and blood, looking more like larva than a future citizen of the world.

They haven't yet decided on a name. This aspect they must ascribe to him even before he has a chance to suggest a theory of what it all means. His gelatinous body must bear a name, have an identity, get rigged out with small iron bars that define him from an early age and integrate him into the community we have agreed to call "the bizarre adventure" of which we're all a part.

The couple is discussing the legitimacy of unisex clothes. At the table over a quickly made dinner, baby in her arms, Madrassa Chauveau jokes that everyone should understand how uncomfortable having big breasts can be. Her jovial husband delivers a few dirty jokes, quite acceptable at the time though no longer tolerated or considered funny today, then goes back to greedily shovelling

Shirriff instant mashed potatoes into his mouth, while his wife, struck by an idea, says without any preamble:

—Claude, we should call him Claude! Isn't that the best unisex name?

Mr. Chauveau—a devil's envoy of universal culture, newly hired civil servant, Odanak reserve headband in his hair—doesn't find it too original, wants something more distinct, that makes more of a statement.

Madrassa, full of the literary knowledge she acquired in her lit degree at Université de Montréal, blushes and brazenly points her finger at her young husband. She has a strange idea:

—He'll be the only one in Quebec, no one would ever give their child this name, just us. You want something rare, meaningful, you wanna make an impression, show off with your kid's name? OK, check this out! It's far out. Tiresias. We'll call him Tiresias!

—(*Caught between irritation and excitement*) Huh, what're you talking about? Where'd you hear that crazy name?

—We'll call him Tiresias, daddy-o, it'll get everyone talking!

On the radio, at very low volume, the arrangements on the Hammond B3 organ of "Crystal Blue Persuasion" by Tommy James & the Shondells crackles in the night air. Something beats on an organic membrane, a rhythmic, ruling, trippy music. It's just a vague entreaty, a bit of normal hope, nothing too unsettling.

Josiane, 2012—Phone call

Josiane taps the green icon on her cell. Grouchy eyes, creaking mattress, stale formalin breath. A call in the middle of the night, at an hour of bad news.

One minute is all it takes to announce a person's death. Including phatic utterances like "hello" and rhetorical phrases such as "may I speak with." This kind of news requires only a very short preamble.

The French language has very few words to express the courtesies of mourning. It has even fewer words to celebrate someone's birth. One stops at the customary "congratulations." All the particularities of mourning or birth, the two essential mysteries, are experienced in the unique, idiomatic register of each person.

Josiane taps the red icon.

Gratitude is so brief, the impact of others on our fugitive bodies so invasive. All of us, relegated to our various prisons with pink, red, black, grey, transparent walls, walls made of cloth, thin glass, plastic, stacked packs of bulldozers. All of us, awaiting the nth escape, craving the endorphins, adrenaline, serotonin, substances that reinvent our feeling of freedom every time.

Evelyne has just hung up. Her right hand set down the handset of the telephone in the Neptune Room. A few days ago, she placed in her pocket a short list of numbers to call at the fateful moment. A dozen names.

It is difficult for Josiane to measure the sorrow that comes over her. Visiting vulnerable people who otherwise have so much zest for life is heartbreaking. The equation *vulnerability + zest for life* causes chaotic chemical reactions in her. Josiane cries discreetly but regularly. Faced with the futile tragedy of a deadly disease, it is touching to meet people still capable of boundless love, a bright smile, always on the case, teeming with words to say. This naïveté, of gleaming pureness, strikes down the dragon of cynics in the world, destabilizes, unsettles, violently whips all fatalistic comments. At the end of life, naïveté, previously disparaged, worn thin, ridiculed, pilloried by realist thought, becomes a weapon. The last weapon against constrictive common sense.

Josiane holds back one or two sighs, a breathing reflex engaged as soon as we feel sorrow. Which is normal. Because we always mourn several things at the same time. She mourns for Sandrine's courage, her tragic fate, her contagious enthusiasm, but also for her own lack of courage, the incredible banality of her life, and her inability to love with a fervour as generous as that of the unparalleled little dancer, her favourite Automatiste choreographer.

Evelyne has invited Josiane to be part of the receiving line for Sandrine.

She will be there, just before noon, at the entrance to the Emily Dickinson Home. To pay tribute to the last of the unknown soldiers on the front line.

Remains holder, 2012

The large black body bag.

   Mass of infinity.

   Remains holder.

The technicians close the thick, opaque plastic over Sandrine's bare body. Besides the shuffling of feet in ankle boots, only the light murmur of the zipper moving on its minuscule teeth hangs in the air. No one breathes a word.

   Their throats on strike. Grafted.

   To a wordless, rocky outcrop.

Puncto reflexionis, 2012

Tiresias gets off the 191 bus in Stoney Point Park, Lachine.

In front of hir, of them, of em, of Shim stands a monument to those who died in the First World War, a bronze soldier on a base. The sun caresses its contours.

The banks of Lake Saint-Louis are lined with 0"–¾" gravel and ½" river rocks, dotted by tufts of tall green grass, leafy bushes, and ample amounts of plantain growing out of the rocky areas and giving the space with its lawn and commemorative poplars the semblance of a grey beach that doesn't claim to be beautiful but tries to be practical.

A fluvial lake, a basin fed by the spillway of the Beauharnois Canal, Lake Saint-Louis holds in its depths and along its shores the steel hulls of ships from the Great Lakes and the remaining traces of polluted areas. Until 1992, the factories and businesses around the lake dumped their sewage into it, leaving an indelible mark on its marine life.

The entity with diminished eyesight and astounding willpower advances toward Lisette Lemieux's work. A large steel panel framing the river. Tiresias is alone on this late August morning of 2012, hardly bothered by the fast cyclists, quickly fleeing out of sight in their helmets and racing shorts, beneath which applauded vigour and physical exertion pulsate. Green highways now traverse slow parks.

For Tiresias, the only time frame that still exists is that of escape. E has adjusted eir battery to the hour of peace. Some kind of return is possible, there must be a way back, Shim is sure of it as e skirts around the work cut out of industrial material, a steel frame on which the letters FLEUVE spell river on the horizon. Perhaps the most constant and most necessary word to understanding everything. An ideal metaphorical tool, the Swiss army knife of writers, the same old tune and powerful visage.

Tiresias's body is a vibrating explosion, an inability to go in circles, a peace treaty with the world, against the madness of passports and the coarseness of financial trappings. More than the "scramble suit" of a million identities in Philip K. Dick's *A Scanner Darkly*, eir mass is a natural solution, a reasonable happenstance relieving the world of its noxious tensions, offering an excessive response to the general dissatisfaction.

We are death's handiwork, the constant depravity of destiny.

Junk cells in a bazaar of epiphany.

Frantic repetitions of shocking passions preparing for nowhere.

The molecules in Tiresias's body have rebelled.

The molecules in the world are rebelling.

The entity whose form is gradually evolving no longer resembles a humanoid shape with a clear outline.

Tiresias becomes Retisias, Sasitire, Risiates, Taisseri, Taissire, Aitiress.

Tiresias becomes the final memory, embodying it like a living hologram.

Receiving line, 2012

At the entrance to the Emily Dickinson Home, a receiving line.

A few people paying tribute to the passing of Sandrine's last body. The last version of herself, frozen in a dry lake with sharp sediments, food for the soil that won't feed any soil.

Tiresias, the charge nurse, Josiane, Aïsha Riyad, and Evelyne stand on either side of the mnemonic current. Other employees of the centre complete the line.

At a certain moment, they applaud, hands tapping the hot July air, jostling it, making clapping sounds with ancient echoes. At once, history is reborn, and hundreds of temporal puncta remind them that one perceives everything on a continuum, that there aren't a hundred thousand points in a life, but a single life, complete both upstream and downstream, a delirious refuge of affections. They then take some time to embrace one another.

Both halves of the door to the mortuary van close.

It's for the best that people disperse.

That the clutches of the past finally let go of the suffering.

Puncto reflexionis, 2012

You just need to disappear, s/he, they, e, Shim, the entity tells emself.

You just need to throw in the towel, chuck the desire for failure into the blue of the sky. Tiresias moves toward the shore. The brownish water over a rocky bed of Lake Saint-Louis, a lunar landscape submerged in dishwater.

Not to kill emself, but to slip through the interstices of the ultimate simulation, escape others' permanent scrutiny, reject violence, aggression, the cycles of life/death, gender/oppression, privilege/oppression, beauty/ oppression, race/oppression, intelligence/oppression, money/ oppression, boredom/oppression, criticism/oppression. Leave the opprobrium machine, the integrated circuits of automatic prejudice, the stock market of ideas, and the normative, repetitive races against time. Not to let go, but to disappear as a result, eliminating all trace, rejecting sociopathic survival, reverting to majority rule, to a total disappearance of the self.

The lapping foam and whoosh of the waves reach Tiresias's shoes. The entity breathes with the solemnity of works that create peddlers of marvels in the imagination. The day is mild, ordinary. There's no reason for disappearing today, there are never enough arguments for distancing oneself from the occasional exhilaration of pleasure, not everything is rosy but it's not black either, only a russet beige, a grey spreading on a clear sabayon. No one has reason to leave, no one has reason to stay. We fiddle with the elements, the foam pleases us, stuns us, spurs us into action, petrifies us, makes us suffer, drives stakes into our hands: all religions dictate that we must go on.

Stupid hogwash.

In Japanese culture, disappearance is permitted, or at least tolerated. There, if financial or existential problems consume your last reasons for dragging your ruinous identity along, you can choose to disappear, change your life. You then become a *johatsu*, an "evaporated person."

From liquid, you turn into gas. Incognito. Your parcel of life migrates to another state, you can choose to no longer be who you are.

The only real freedom worth anything is the freedom to no longer be yourself, change your life, try on another suit from the shop of appearances.

Tiresias's de-evolutionary pilgrimage

In Lake Saint-Louis, Tiresias begins the only atheist pilgrimage possible.

Head underwater, e slowly reaches the basin's maximum depth, at the level of the seaway. Silt, algae, pike, chunks of concrete, all kinds of dead branches, bits of civilization, vast marine landscape, hidden forest, the bottom of Lake Saint-Louis harbours mysteries whose scope only a patient walker could define.

As eir body delves deeper into the liquid mass, hair like wild algae, shirt stuck to the body, ashy smouldering eyes, Tiresias de-evolves, adapts to the water's dark, liquefied silence. Gills grow along eir sides, eir ears contract, eir nostrils tumefy then retract, eir T-shirt starts constricting eir breathing. In the water's depths, the sun emits luminous memories rather than bright light. Everything is veiled in diaphanous blocks. The abandoned T-shirt gets tangled on a scrap of wire fencing stuck in the dense silt.

E follows the silent current, the constant speed, the energetic capacity of molecules, the channel of goods, the channel of marine life, the Saint Lawrence Seaway. The muffled drone of all types of engines, the marine roofs of long steel cigars, ferries, and container ships, vessels of darkness for deep-sea inhabitants, hammer their presence past the Port of Montreal. In Lake Saint-Pierre, a large platter of water with a twenty-metre trench at its centre for ships, Tiresias keeps walking toward the estuary. The marine life gradually changes, the species become more diverse, the ceiling gets lower. A few times, e passes shell casings, remnants of conflicts and military exercises, powerful symbols of time passing beyond the liquid realm. Half of the lake has served as a training area for national defence. Domination is always a national action, an identity-based action. To dominate, you need to be someone.

Hours and hours and hours that Tiresias no longer counts. Hours frightened away by their own unsuitability to the perpetual, subdued grey night of the seabed.

Arriving at the southern channel, running along Île d'Orléans, the entity begins to change form, eir hands become attached to eir body, eir face loses all recognizable features and is covered by a thick gelatin of spongy whiteness. Near Les Escoumins, at a depth of more than three hundred metres, without light, eir feet still pounding the kilometres, Tiresias passes starfish, crenellated nudibranchs, giant mussels, *Gorgonocephalus*, sea cucumbers, scarlet *Psolus*, sea urchins, sea potatoes, an entire vivarium up to now unknown to eir comprehension, which already doesn't analyze things as a function of tomorrow, blind to the present of all species, detached from the constant injection of information about everyone's angst. Near Les Escoumins, Tiresias's feet choose, without consulting em, because eir body stopped consulting em a long time ago, a huge stray boulder teeming with northern *Terebratula*—fossilized brachiopods, something like smaller versions of the great scallop with cilia and valves for filtering plankton. On this rocky outcrop, at a depth of more than two hundred metres, eir legs become a single peduncle that attaches itself to the substrate.

Of Tiresias, only the "T" remains.

A letter drill, an umbrella.

Time passes and passes and passes. An interlude for no reason. A year later, at the right moment, determined by factors beyond human understanding, a strobilation process begins.

The "T" of Tiresias reproduces its own progeny; the underwater polyp becomes the scientific polyp, the reproducing polyp. Without semen or fornication, in an autonomous, asexual manner, from the base to the top of the polyp, strobilation carries out its work, accumulating clones in its own language.

This is how the lion's mane jellyfish, the *Cyanea capillata* of the Saint Lawrence Estuary, reproduces. Without needing the problematic encounter between two inconsistent desires, entirely self-sufficient, without the burden of consciousness that trains us to be responsible for everything.

Transparent palms floating mid-water, one jellyfish after another breaks away from the polyp in search of food.

The music of the living strums its strings once more.

In the dark, watery depths, beneath the world's appalling mountain of problems, a young jellyfish drifts away.

Its solitary life begins.

Its death doesn't concern anyone.

Acknowledgments

Thank you to Martin Winckler, for his open mind and medical humanism, which greatly inspired me. Johanne Desrochers, Director of the Maison André-Gratton, for taking my wild notions of realism seriously. Justine Jaran-Duquette, for kindly taking the time to show me around the premises. Lynne Cayouette, for the impromptu conversation in the centre's corridors, which ultimately gave me a scene. And the entire team of the Maison André-Gratton—tremendous, generous, attentive, devoted—thanks to which this humanist work celebrating a child's life, giving it its due respect to the very end, demonstrates the vital contribution of pediatric palliative care to our society.

A translator's pilgrimage/A translation's evolution

In the estuary between *La chambre neptune* and *The Neptune Room*, a translator embarks on one among many possible pilgrimages.

Submerging, the translator gradually reaches the novel's maximum depth, at the level of an interstitial seaway. Meanings, historical contexts, cultural references, subjective emotions, echoes of grammars, all kinds of temporalities, speculative fragments, relative densities, vast semantic ecosystems, divergent interpretations of being all navigate the bottom of the estuary, whose scope expands and contracts to the rhythm of the translator's perambulations.

As the body delves deeper into the linguistic mass, the translation evolves, adapts to the ideas and voices of *la chambre*, but also to the contours and currents of *the room's* present historical moment. As such, inevitable change occurs; some of the names transform into their English counterparts (which are never quite equivalent); key words such as *flickering* undergo extensive consideration; eccentricities are translated into idiosyncrasies; French references become more opaque; English references become more obvious; the gender treatment of Tiresias, rare and rebellious in French yet too constrictive if rendered identically in English, expands into an exploration of gender pronouns across eras. In the novel's depths, the time (and all the situated meaning woven into it) of its writing and the time (and all the relocated meaning extracted from it) of its translation are not the same, are never static. To achieve a translucent spectrum of the novel's tangles and dense silt, the radicalism control knob is turned a couple of notches higher.

Still, the translator follows the voicing current, the constant speed, the energetic capacity of morphemes, the channel of morphological life, the interstitial seaway of the novel's reverberations. All the while listening to the drone of all types of syntactical engines—vessels of possibility for the inhabitants and concepts of any language hammering their presence past the Port of la Chambre Neptune.

MONTREAL-BASED BERTRAND LAVERDURE is a poet, novelist, and literary performer. He has published six novels, including *Universal Bureau of Copyrights* (2014) and *Readopolis* (2017), both translated by Oana Avasilichioaei. His many poetry publications include *Cascadeuse* (2013) and *Sept et demi* (2007). He was awarded the Joseph S. Stauffer Prize from the Canada Council for the Arts (1999) and the Rina Lasnier Prize for Poetry (2003) for *Les forêts* (2000). He was a literary chronicler on MAtv and CIBL Radio, and Poet Laureate of Montreal from 2015 to 2017.

PHOTO: PAM DICK

MONTREAL-BASED POET, TRANSLATOR, and artist Oana Avasilichioaei has published six poetry collections, including *Eight Track* (2019), *Limbinal* (2015), and *We, Beasts* (2012, winner, A. M. Klein Prize for Poetry). She has translated many books of poetry and prose, including Catherine Lalonde's *The Faerie Devouring* (2018, winner, Cole Foundation Prize for Translation), Bertrand Laverdure's *Readopolis* (2017, winner, Governor General's Literary Award for Translation), and Daniel Canty's *Wigrum* (2013). For more about Oana, visit oanalab.com.

Colophon

Manufactured as the first English
edition of *The Neptune Room* in the
summer of 2020 by Book*hug Press

Copy edited by Stuart Ross
Type + design by Malcolm Sutton

bookhugpress.ca

Book*hug Press